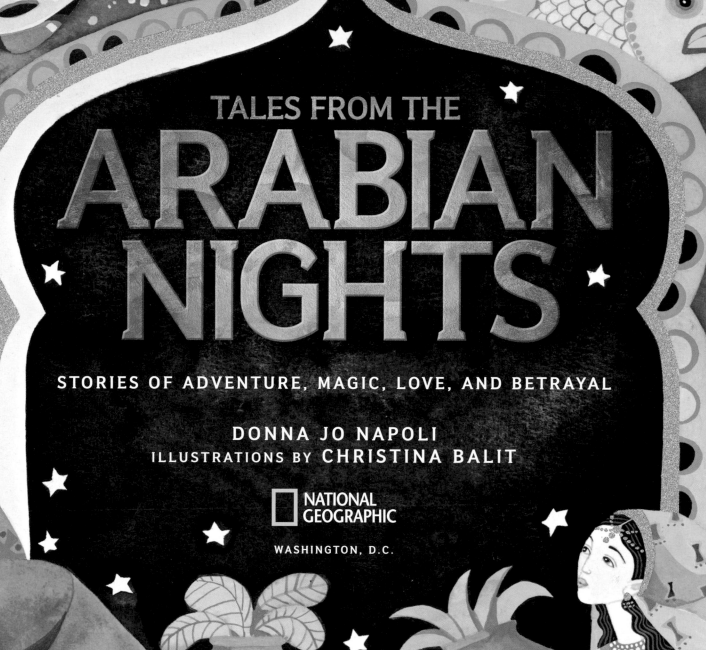

TALES FROM THE
ARABIAN NIGHTS

STORIES OF ADVENTURE, MAGIC, LOVE, AND BETRAYAL

DONNA JO NAPOLI
ILLUSTRATIONS BY CHRISTINA BALIT

NATIONAL GEOGRAPHIC

WASHINGTON, D.C.

THE TALES

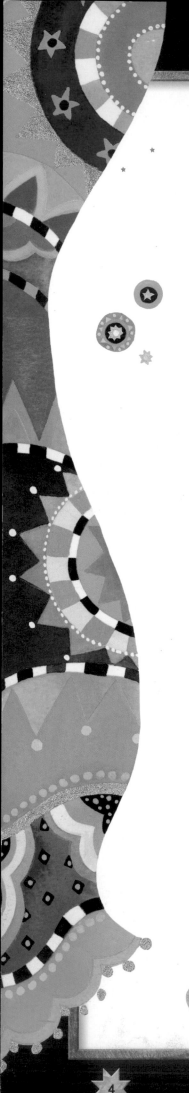

Some of the stories presented in this book go back to ancient times; others may have arisen in medieval times. Most appeared in collections during the Middle Ages; others were first written down only at the beginning of the 18th century by a European translator of the earlier collections. Probably all, however, were part of folklore of the area extending from North Africa to South Asia—including Mesopotamian, Persian, and Indian cultures, as well as later medieval Muslim cultures of Egypt and Syria. As such, these stories offer an entrance to the sensibilities of that wide area in those varying times.

The society we find in these stories consists of many poor, undereducated people, scrambling to stay within the good graces of a wealthy upper class that holds the power. Wealth, however, does not seem to be strictly random. Instead, those who work hard and are clever enough to seize opportunities can rise from poverty to luxury as merchants or even become viziers, princes, and kings. Self-reliance and resourcefulness are prized qualities.

The supernatural beings that inhabit these stories are also a mixed bag of beneficent and maleficent. Woe to the human who just happens to offend a jinni by accident; mercy is a rare find. (Please note that the Arabic word *jinni* is used in this book, with the plural form *jinn,* and the feminine form *jinniya.* Often in English it is spelled *genie,* which is the more common transliteration of the Arabic spelling.) But a rapid assessment of a situation—particularly of the psychological needs of the one in power—and careful, appropriate action can lead to the mere human prevailing over the magical creature so that disaster is avoided. And generally, those who are loyal and faithful fare better than those who are not.

Finally, there is an abiding interest in exploration and invention. Adventurers go from country to country, risking their lives in order to see the world. New machines are treasured. There is nothing complacent or provincial in these stories. Rather, there is a hunger for the unknown and a desire to be part of something larger.

In these ways, the values and beliefs reflected in the stories feel optimistic—to my way of thinking, more so than those found in ancient or medieval Greek, Norse, Celtic, or ancient Egyptian mythology. There is a strong sense that good behavior will lead to good results and that the world is basically a lot more delightful than it is frightful.

A remarkable aspect of these particular tales is the structure of how they are told. There is an overall framework in which a wife, Scheherazade, is telling stories to her husband each night. But in the stories she tells, there is often a character who tells a story. And sometimes we find another story within that embedded story—stories within stories within stories within the overarching story. Now, certainly, the current form of the framework of Scheherazade was not there in the original oral folktales. But even having three layers of storytelling within the individual oral tales is a lot to keep track of—it is as complex to the ear as Persian miniature paintings, for example, are to the eye. This storytelling tradition puts an emphasis on careful listening and mental jockeying. The listener is rewarded frequently by gifts to the ear—songs and poems—as well as gifts to the spirit: characters who make us laugh, love stories that hold us entranced, fantastical creatures and devices that amaze us. For the people of the times when the stories were first told, historical details shed light on events they might have heard about.

Each night's tale stands on its own merit. But I have worked to present them within the framework of a growing relationship between wife and husband. The tales themselves are often cliffhangers that leave us wondering what will happen next. But the most important cliffhanger is whether or not Scheherazade succeeds in getting her husband to grant her another day of life—for in the beginning, he has vowed to have her put to death after their first night together. This innocent girl is subject to the whims of a man so deeply wounded his ego wobbles with every step. Scheherazade uses all her story-telling skills, ingenuity, and artistic creativity to craft stories that make her husband's heart beat faster. But she also selects stories with an eye toward developing a sense of trust and, eventually, mercy built on that trust. This helps her husband to move beyond his injury to the strength and hope that allow him to experience profound love. Scheherazade wins not through trickery, but through understanding human nature, and through faith in her own abilities and in the transformative power of storytelling. She dares to fathom the meaning of life with every bit of intelligence she has. As a result, she embodies the spirit of the times and places of the tales she spins.

Welcome to that spirit.

THE TALE OF SHAH RAYAR & SHAH ZAMAN

Two brothers were kings. Shah Rayar, the older, ruled the land beyond the Indus River. Shah Zaman, the younger, ruled the land of Samarqand.

One day Shah Rayar missed his brother. He sent his adviser, his vizier, to fetch him.

Shah Zaman happily prepared horses and camels with supplies for the journey. But the night before leaving, he found his wife romancing a kitchen boy. Shah Zaman cried, then got furious. How could she! He was a shah—a ruler! He put them to death.

When Shah Zaman arrived at his brother's home, he kept thinking of his secret disgrace. He couldn't eat. He couldn't sleep.

Shah Rayar decided a hunt might cheer him up. But Shah Zaman refused to go. So Shah Rayar left without him.

Shah Zaman sat and moaned when—what was that?—his brother's wife strutted across the garden with servant girls. They stopped below Shah Zaman's window, so close he could see that some were girls, yes, but others were boys! They kissed and tangled together.

How awful! His brother's wife was worse than his own! But, oh, this was the way of the world. Shah Zaman no longer felt singled out for misery. He ate that evening; he slept that night.

When Shah Rayar returned, he found his brother recovered. "What blight caused you to fade before?"

Shah Zaman didn't want to answer. But Shah Rayar insisted. So Shah Zaman told what his own wife had done.

"I condemned them both."

Shah Rayar gasped. "Good! Tell me now how you recovered."

PREVIOUS PAGES:

Shah Zaman secretly watched his brother's wife and her servants in the garden. Alas, his brother had been betrayed, just as Shah Zaman had been betrayed. Wives were wicked.

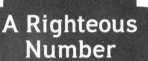

A Righteous Number

Four antique books are stacked together on a desk.

Four is the righteous number in many ancient Islamic cultures. The ear needs four instruments for the best music: lute, harp, zither, and double flute. The nose needs four flowers for the best scents: rose, myrtle, anemone, and gillyflower. The soul needs four books for support: Torah, Psalms, the Gospel, and the Koran. A table needs four legs for support. A man can take four wives (or fewer). The list goes on. Other cultures that revere four include Byzantine, Celtic, Chinese, Etruscan, Hindu, Hopi, Maya, Navajo, and Lakota.

Again Shah Zaman didn't want to answer. Again Shah Rayar insisted. So Shah Zaman told what his brother's wife had done.

Shah Rayar was stunned. He had to see for himself. They announced another hunt, and left immediately. But then they snuck back, and spied on the queen and her servants frolicking again.

Shah Rayar ripped at his hair. Nothing could be counted on. He no longer wanted this life. The brothers agreed to wander as vagabonds. Only if they met someone with misfortunes greater than theirs would they return.

They stopped near the shore. A roar came from the water. The brothers hid in a tree. A demon jinni, tall as a pillar, broad as a camel, sloshed out of the sea. On his head balanced a glass chest with four locks. The jinni opened it, and lifted out a woman.

"Gorgeous wife, I need sleep." He laid his head on her lap and his snores rumbled the earth.

The woman saw the brothers in the tree. She insisted they roll on the ground with her. "Give me your rings," she said. The men each gave her a ring. She opened a purse and shook out more rings: Turkish gold, Egyptian silver, Ethiopian ivory, blue lapis lazuli, and bloodred carnelian. "Now I have exactly one from each man I have romanced as this jinni slept. That's what he gets for locking me up."

The brothers ran off. The jinni's wife was wicked—like all women. They vowed never to marry again and they returned home. Shah Rayar condemned his wife and her servants to death.

He thought about the beautiful woman in the chest, and his insides twisted in confusion. He didn't want to risk the pain a wife brought. Yet he needed a wife, for love between husband and wife helps mortals reach for the Almighty. So that night he made his terrible vow: From thence forward, Shah Rayar would marry daily, and the next morning he would have his bride slain.

The poor vizier spent each day finding a new bride for Shah Rayar. And all perished. Parents mourned, for their daughters were not wicked. No. Their daughters were gentle people. Every breath of joy in the kingdom died. ✴

THE TALES OF THE DONKEY, THE OX & THE MERCHANTS

The vizier's daughters were Scheherazade and Dinarzad.
Scheherazade studied philosophy, literature, medicine. She recited
poetry. She understood the lessons of history. And she had a giant heart.
She looked around at the daily slaughter of girls, at the grief of parents,
and that heart broke. "Father, I will marry Shah Rayar and
I will save the people or die trying." The vizier argued with her.
Scheherazade insisted. The vizier grew angry. Scheherazade
grew intransigent. The vizier shouted, "What happened to the
donkey and the ox with the merchant will happen to you!"
"What happened to them?" So the vizier told this tale.

A merchant could understand animal language. He kept what he heard secret, however, for he feared if he told, he'd die.

One day he heard the ox say to the donkey, "You're lucky to live in a swept stall, with cool drinking water and sifted barley to eat. Your only work is carrying the merchant on errands. But me, I pull a plow all day. The yoke cuts my neck. I slurp muddy water, gobble dirty beans, and sleep in filth."

"Rebel," said the donkey. "Lie down and moan."

After that the ox wouldn't budge. He wouldn't eat. He lay on his back. The merchant, who expected this, told the plowman to yoke the donkey instead.

So the donkey pulled the load. Meanwhile, the ox chewed cud. That night when the donkey returned exhausted and bleeding, the ox thanked him for such good advice.

The vizier looked at his generous but headstrong daughter.
He couldn't bear the thought of that head on Shah Rayar's
pillow … and what would happen to it later. "See? For the sake of
everything holy, Daughter, don't expose yourself to peril."
Scheherazade had thought about the dilemma nonstop.
She was smart, so she had to try. "I must."

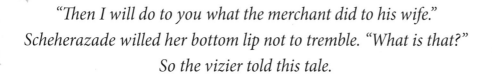

"Then I will do to you what the merchant did to his wife."
Scheherazade willed her bottom lip not to tremble. "What is that?"
So the vizier told this tale.

The merchant overheard the donkey and ox talking. "You must change again," said the donkey. "If you stay bad, the merchant said he'll butcher you to feed the poor and make your hide a rug."

The stupid ox bellowed and farted. "I will!"

The merchant laughed at the donkey's cleverness.

His wife drew back. "Are you laughing at me?"

"I'm laughing at what the donkey said."

"What did he say?"

"I'll die if I tell you."

But the woman insisted. So the merchant had no choice. Before telling, though, he prepared for death. He wrote a will and bade farewell to all. Just then he overheard his dog and rooster talking. The rooster had been chasing hens. The dog scolded him for playing when the merchant was about to die. The rooster scoffed. "The merchant's a fool. I tame these hens—with brute force—just one of me and so many of them. He has but one wife, yet she wins. He should tame her."

The merchant immediately battled with his wife until she said she no longer wanted to know what the donkey had said.

So the merchant didn't tell, and he didn't die.

Scheherazade's eyelids went heavy with pity for her father. "You won't battle with me, Father," she said gently, "for I can't change my mind." Before Scheherazade left home, she told Dinarzad that she would send for her that night. "And, Little Sister, you must find the right moment to ask me to tell a tale." Dinarzad nodded agreement through a veil of tears. That night, when Shah Rayar took Scheherazade to his royal chambers, she told the king she needed to bid farewell to her sister. So the king sent for Dinarzad, who crawled under their bed and slept. ✷

OPPOSITE:
The merchant eavesdropped on his animals. He heard the rooster tell the dog that the merchant was a fool. The merchant should boss his wife around, like the rooster bossed the hens.

13

THE TALE OF THE MERCHANT & THE JINNI

At midnight, Dinarzad woke and said, "Sister, if you are not sleepy, would you tell me a tale—one of your wonderful tales—to while away the time till daybreak, when I must bid you farewell?" Scheherazade turned to the king. "May I?" The king was now fully awake, so why not indulge his bride in the last hours of her life? So Scheherazade began to spin a tale, slowly slowly, lingering on each detail, savoring every word as though it were her last.

A wealthy merchant journeyed on horseback to a far land. On his way home, he sat by a spring and ate dates, throwing the pits away. All at once a jinni appeared, so tall his head was bathed in clouds. He carried a gigantic sword. "You killed my son! Stand and I will kill you now."

The merchant denied that he had ever done such a thing.

But the jinni insisted. His son was walking by when one of the merchant's date pits struck and killed him. "You must die," said the jinni. "Blood for blood."

The merchant begged for mercy. The jinni offered none. The merchant recited poetry to soften the jinni's resolve. The jinni only raised his sword.

The merchant begged permission to go home and set his affairs in order. He would need until New Year's Day to attend to it all, after which he swore to return. The jinni agreed.

The merchant's family wailed and wept at his impending doom. The merchant gritted his teeth. He divided his properties among his older children, appointed guardians for his younger children, and gave alms to the poor. Then he got on his horse

with his burial shroud in his arms, and traveled to the jinni's orchard, arriving on the first day of the new year.

He sat on the ground and waited. A venerable old man—a sheikh—came along, leading a gazelle on a leash. The sheikh asked the merchant what he was waiting for, so the merchant told his tale. The sheikh's jaw fell open at the fact that the merchant had returned as promised. Not many were that faithful. He waited with the merchant to see what would happen next.

As the merchant and the sheikh with the gazelle were talking, another sheikh approached with two black dogs in tow. He asked why they were sitting there. So the sheikh with the gazelle told the merchant's story, and how he had returned as promised so that the jinni could kill him.

The sheikh with the two black dogs stared at the merchant. Such fidelity was incredible. He swore not to leave until he saw how the adventure ended. So he sat beside the merchant and the sheikh with the gazelle, and all three of them talked.

A third sheikh wandered up now. A mule walked at his side. When he heard why they were sitting there, he too sat down and swore not to leave until he saw what the jinni did to the merchant.

The air grew dusty. In an instant, they were sitting in a cloud of dust and the earth shook under them.

The giant jinni appeared. "Get ready to die."

The three old men made a chorus of weeping. The gazelle blinked. The two black dogs whined. The mule stamped in place.

And the merchant trembled.

Dawn entered through the window and Scheherazade lapsed into silence. She trembled like the merchant of her story.
"What a marvelous tale," said Dinarzad.
"It's nothing compared with what I shall tell tomorrow, if the king spares me one more night." Scheherazade stayed her breath to hear the king's response.
Shah Rayar wanted to know what would happen to the merchant, for surely a man who had killed by accident should be spared. Even a jinni could recognize that. But injustices happened in this world—as he knew too well. "Yes, you can continue another night."
Scheherazade breathed again. She would live another day.
She gulped the air. ✳

THE TALE OF
THE FIRST SHEIKH

*At midnight the next night, Dinarzad called, "Sister, wake
and continue that tale." Scheherazade was awake, of course.
She turned to the king, who stirred beside her. "May I?"
The king assented. Scheherazade began fast, before this
all-powerful man could change his mind.*

The jinni stood his ground, while the merchant sobbed. The first
sheikh, the one with the gazelle, kissed the jinni's feet.
"King of jinn-kings," he said, "I have a tale. If you find it more fabulous
than what happened between you and the merchant, will you grant
me one-third of your right to the merchant's life?"

The jinni agreed.

The first sheikh told this tale.

~

THIS GAZELLE IS MY WIFE. I LOVED HER BUT SHE BORE NO CHILDREN.
So I took a second wife, who bore a son. My first wife grew jealous.

One day I left on a yearlong journey. During that time, my first
wife learned magic. She turned my second wife into a cow and my
son into a bull. When I returned, my first wife said my second wife
had died and my son had run off. Bereft, I beat my chest.

When the Great Feast of the Immolation came, I asked my
animal tender to bring me a cow for sacrifice. The chosen cow
mooed piteously, as though she understood she was to die. She was
my second wife—but I knew nothing. Still, her eyes pleaded. So I
asked for a different cow. But my first wife insisted on butchering
that cow.

The cow's insides were nothing but bones and nerves. No flesh,
no fat. What a waste to have butchered her! I told my animal tender
to fetch a fat young bull now. The bull rubbed his head against my
chest and lowed sweetly. Little did I know he was my son. Still, my
insides panged. "Pick a different bull," I told the animal tender. But
my first wife said, "Butcher this one!" So I gripped the knife. After
all, my first wife was all I had.

Animal Sacrifices

*Two cows graze together at
dawn on the Lower Galilee.*

Ceremonies in which
animals are sacrificed are
common to many religions
throughout history and
around the globe.
Sometimes the sacrifices
are meant to appease an
angry god; other times
they are meant to show
gratitude. The feast talked
about here is a celebration
of the end of the pilgrimage season when pilgrims
and other Muslims sacrifice
animals to affirm their
obedience to and love of
God. The meat of the
sacrificed animals is eaten
by family and friends and
given to the poor.

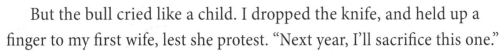

OPPOSITE:

In a fit of jealousy, the first sheikh's first wife turned his son and second wife into cattle. A magician rescued the son from his enchantment and turned the first wife into a gazelle.

But the bull cried like a child. I dropped the knife, and held up a finger to my first wife, lest she protest. "Next year, I'll sacrifice this one."

Later the animal tender whispered to me. His daughter knew magic. She had recognized the bull as my son! In an instant, she guessed the evil my first wife had done.

I offered the girl riches to free my son from the spell. She wanted nothing but to marry him. She sprinkled magic water on him. His body shook hard until there stood my son, strong again!

Then she turned my first wife into this gazelle because a gazelle is beautiful, and we needed to watch her. It is better to look on the beautiful than the ugly.

The first sheikh pet the gazelle gently, for love doesn't disappear even when we wish it would. "Is my tale not fabulous?"

The jinni rubbed the tip of his nose and nodded. "I grant you one-third of my right to this merchant's life." The second sheikh, the one with two black dogs, stood. "I too have a tale. If it is even more fabulous, will you grant me one-third of your right to the merchant's life?"

The jinni agreed.

A shaft of light entered the room. Scheherazade marveled at how day exposed the secrets of the dark. All her life she'd seen dawn come, but only now did she realize this moment— ruled by this first shaft of light—was a revelation. A gem of truth. She feared and loved it, but fear had the lead.
"This tale amazes me," said Dinarzad.
"It will amaze more in the coming night, if the king will allow."
"I will," said Shah Rayar, for his curiosity was piqued. There was not enough air in this room to fill Scheherazade's lungs. She rushed to the window and pushed the shutters wide. ✳

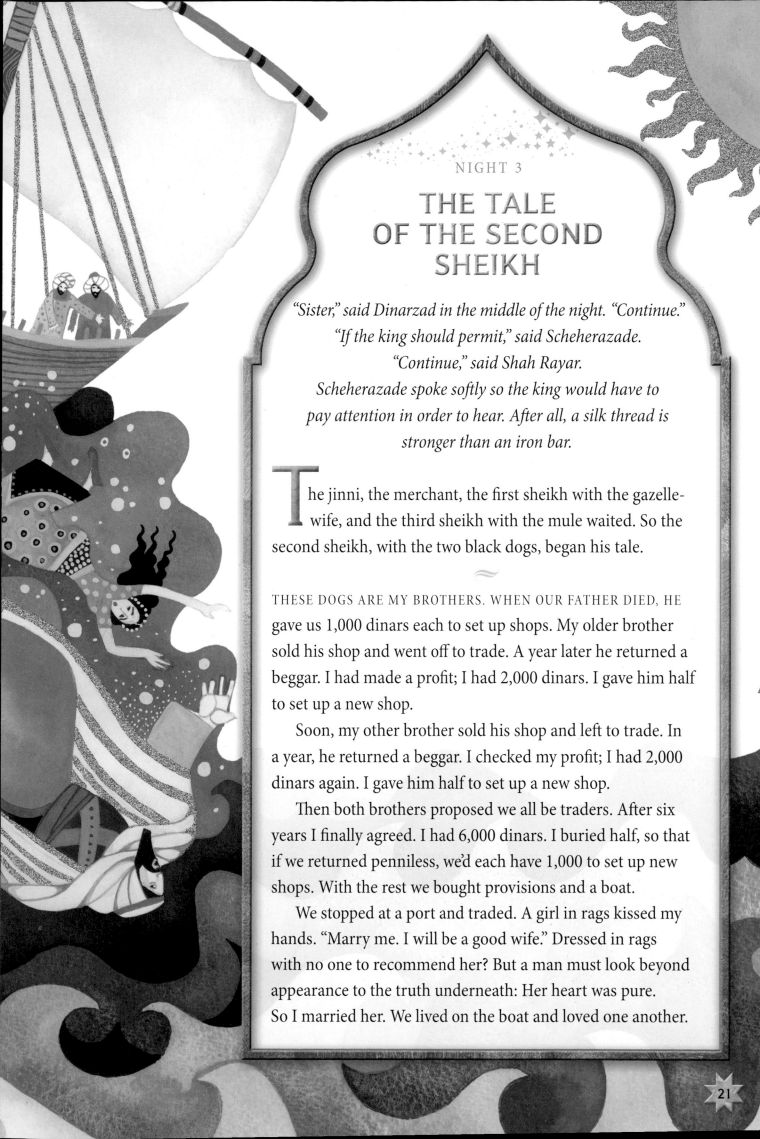

THE TALE OF THE SECOND SHEIKH

"Sister," said Dinarzad in the middle of the night. "Continue."
"If the king should permit," said Scheherazade.
"Continue," said Shah Rayar.
Scheherazade spoke softly so the king would have to
pay attention in order to hear. After all, a silk thread is
stronger than an iron bar.

The jinni, the merchant, the first sheikh with the gazelle-wife, and the third sheikh with the mule waited. So the second sheikh, with the two black dogs, began his tale.

THESE DOGS ARE MY BROTHERS. WHEN OUR FATHER DIED, HE gave us 1,000 dinars each to set up shops. My older brother sold his shop and went off to trade. A year later he returned a beggar. I had made a profit; I had 2,000 dinars. I gave him half to set up a new shop.

Soon, my other brother sold his shop and left to trade. In a year, he returned a beggar. I checked my profit; I had 2,000 dinars again. I gave him half to set up a new shop.

Then both brothers proposed we all be traders. After six years I finally agreed. I had 6,000 dinars. I buried half, so that if we returned penniless, we'd each have 1,000 to set up new shops. With the rest we bought provisions and a boat.

We stopped at a port and traded. A girl in rags kissed my hands. "Marry me. I will be a good wife." Dressed in rags with no one to recommend her? But a man must look beyond appearance to the truth underneath: Her heart was pure. So I married her. We lived on the boat and loved one another.

PREVIOUS PAGES:

The second sheikh's brothers were envious of his marriage. They threw him and his wife into the sea. But the wife was a jinniya, who saved her husband, and her sister turned the brothers into dogs.

Life was perfect. That very perfection set aflame envy in my brothers. One night, as we slept, they tossed us into the sea.

I woke on a gulp of salt water, thrashing hopelessly, for I couldn't swim. My wife turned into a jinniya and carried me away. She told me she had loved me at first sight, and so came to me in the guise of a beggar. She loved me even more for marrying her, despite her apparent poverty. Now she would kill my brothers.

"No!" I said. "Kindness is the rule, even to those who wrong you." We argued. At last she agreed to let my brothers live.

She flew me on her back to my old home. I dug up the 3,000 dinars and opened a shop. When I returned home that night, two black dogs waited by my door. My wife's voice came from nowhere, "These are your brothers. My sister cast a spell on them. After 10 years you may go to her to get it lifted." Her voice ceased. She was gone, dear wife.

The second sheikh scratched the dogs behind the ears. "Is my tale not fabulous?"

The jinni rubbed the tip of his nose and nodded. "I grant you one-third of my right to this merchant's life."

The third sheikh, the one with the mule, stood. "I have the most fabulous tale. If you agree, will you grant me one-third of your right to the merchant's life?"

The jinni nodded.

"Listen hard," said the third sheikh.

Morning came and Scheherazade
hushed, though her pulse drummed in her head.
"A marvelous tale," said Dinarzad.
"Tomorrow's will be better," said Scheherazade,
scanning the king's face. "If the king allows."
Shah Rayar agreed. But he could see where the story was going.
It would end soon and he would put Scheherazade to death.
She had turned a one-night marriage into a four-night
marriage. Four was a good number. ✹

THE THIRD SHEIKH'S STORY & THE TALE OF THE FISHERMAN & THE JINNI

Scheherazade was no one's fool. The king's eyes had told her he found the tale predictable and would soon dispose of her. Like ragged clothing. Like rotted meat. Fear dried her mouth. It shortened her breath. All her life her father and neighbors had told tales. All her life she had read and studied. Surely that experience and knowledge would help her create new tales. Surely, oh, surely. The desperate girl wracked her brain. That night, when Dinarzad begged for more, Scheherazade took a giant breath and let it out in one long blast.

The third sheikh, the one with the mule, told his tale.

≈

MY WIFE BETRAYED ME, THEN TURNED ME INTO A DOG. I WENT TO a magician. She rescued me and gave me magic water to sprinkle on my wife. It turned her into a mule, this mule.

≈

"IS THIS NOT A FABULOUS TALE?" HE ASKED. "INDEED." THE JINNI acceded to him one-third of his right to the merchant's life. Of course the three old men together then granted life to the merchant.

The words tumbled from Scheherazade's lips like cascading water. She watched the king's satisfied eyes; he had anticipated this ending. "This tale," she said in that same stream of breath, "is nothing compared to the fisherman's." "Tell," said Dinarzad, "Now!" Dinarzad was, indeed, the finest sister ever. Scheherazade didn't wait for permission; nothing good could come of waiting.

Prayer Times

A Muslim man prays while low light streams in through the window.

The fisherman of this tale is Muslim. He prays five times a day: at dawn, right after noon, in mid-afternoon, at sunset, and at night. The time of prayers is determined by the position of the sun. One of the greatest mathematicians and astronomers of the Middle Ages was the Egyptian Ibn Yunus. He lived in the 10th century and made mathematical tables for timekeeping so that prayer could happen at the right times. He was also a poet.

The fisherman's first haul was a donkey corpse; his second, a jar of sand and water; his third, garbage from others' meals. What a sad day for a hungry man with a hungry family.

Afisherman had a family, but no money. Each day he cast his net precisely four times. Whatever he caught fed his family.

He rose every day at the first call for prayers. One morning it was still so dark, the moon glimmered. The fisherman took his prayer rug with him and left the city before the first call to prayer. Then he waded into the sea up to his waist and cast his net.

When he pulled on the rope, it resisted. His net was so heavy, he couldn't move it! He dove into the water and tugged until finally the haul lay on the shore. When he opened the net, a dead donkey lay there.

The fisherman looked at the stinking corpse and recited verses to calm his heart.

> *A fisherman's net and hook provide*
> *As much as the Almighty's heart is wide.*

He prayed again, for it was now sunrise, then cast his net a second time. When he pulled the rope, it resisted. He dove and tugged. In the net lay a jar full of sand and water. No! The man recited more verses, balm for the heart.

All I seek is one square meal,
enough to make our tummies heal.

He knelt for noon prayers, then waded into the water. Alas, the third catch was useless—broken dishes and bottles, garbage from others' meals. His mouth went sour.

One land is wet, another dry
Justice is low; injustice is high.

The fisherman prayed, for it was mid-afternoon.

"The moon was out when the fisherman began his toils,"
said Scheherazade, "but it has gone to bed for us."
She pulled on her fingers so hard they hurt. "I'll tell more in the
coming night. If the king allows." Shah Rayar worried about
this fisherman, so conscientious in his prayers, yet so poor
in his purse. What bad luck to get a dead donkey, a jar of
sand and water, then, worst of all, garbage.
"Tell more in the coming night," he said. "I insist." ✷

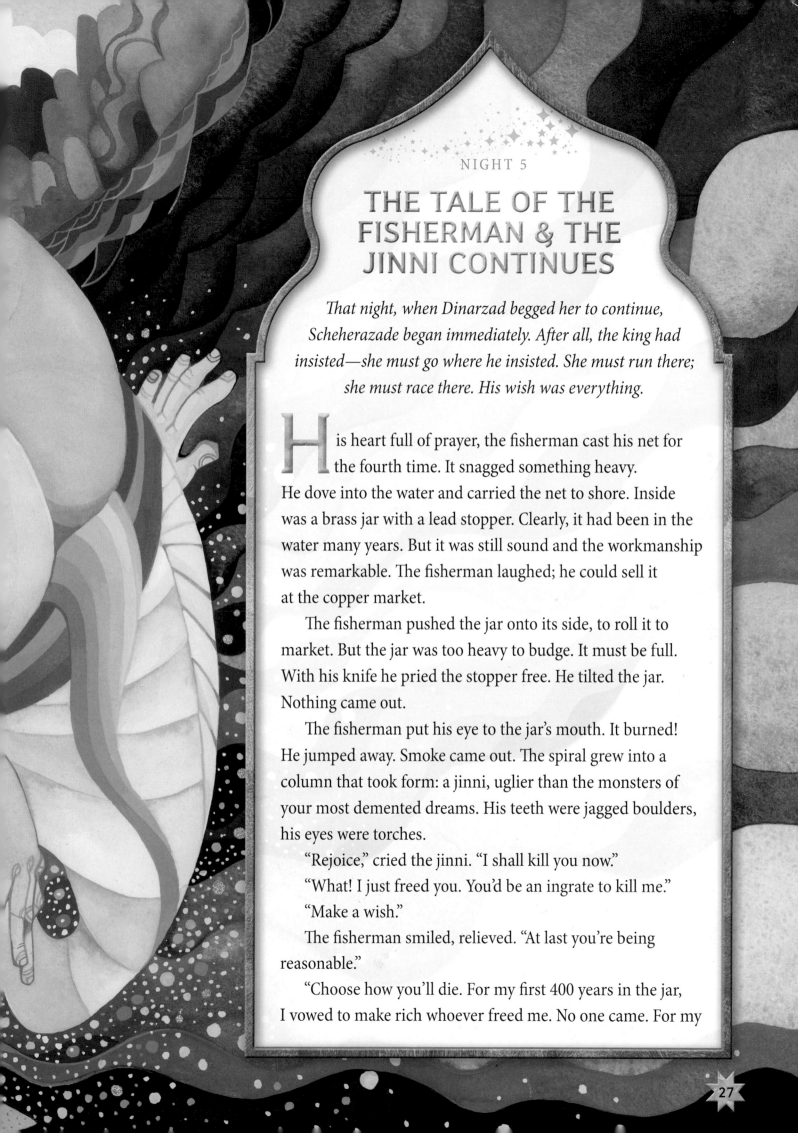

THE TALE OF THE FISHERMAN & THE JINNI CONTINUES

That night, when Dinarzad begged her to continue, Scheherazade began immediately. After all, the king had insisted—she must go where he insisted. She must run there; she must race there. His wish was everything.

His heart full of prayer, the fisherman cast his net for the fourth time. It snagged something heavy. He dove into the water and carried the net to shore. Inside was a brass jar with a lead stopper. Clearly, it had been in the water many years. But it was still sound and the workmanship was remarkable. The fisherman laughed; he could sell it at the copper market.

The fisherman pushed the jar onto its side, to roll it to market. But the jar was too heavy to budge. It must be full. With his knife he pried the stopper free. He tilted the jar. Nothing came out.

The fisherman put his eye to the jar's mouth. It burned! He jumped away. Smoke came out. The spiral grew into a column that took form: a jinni, uglier than the monsters of your most demented dreams. His teeth were jagged boulders, his eyes were torches.

"Rejoice," cried the jinni. "I shall kill you now."

"What! I just freed you. You'd be an ingrate to kill me."

"Make a wish."

The fisherman smiled, relieved. "At last you're being reasonable."

"Choose how you'll die. For my first 400 years in the jar, I vowed to make rich whoever freed me. No one came. For my

PREVIOUS PAGES:

The fisherman's fourth haul was a jar. When he pried open the stopper, out came a jinni who threatened to kill him. But the clever fisherman asked a tricky question first.

next 400 years, I vowed to give every treasure imaginable to whoever freed me. No one came. After that I vowed to make my rescuer a king. No rescuer came. Year after year, no one. Until I decided I would kill whoever freed me. Then you came. Choose how you want to die."

"Please, if you spare me, the Almighty will reward you. If you destroy me, the Almighty will punish you."

"Choose!"

"I choose instead to ask a question," said the fisherman. "Were you really in this jar?"

"You saw I was inside."

"No. I opened the jar and smoke appeared. When it cleared, there you were. But you're too large to fit inside."

"I am not."

They argued, until the jinni jumped into the jar and called out, "See? I fit."

The fisherman jammed the stopper into place.

"No!" wailed the tricked jinni. "Let me out and I'll make you rich."

"You lie," said the fisherman. "You would do to me as Sage Duban did to King Yunan."

"I don't know that story," said the jinni. "Tell it."

Morning warmed Scheherazade's cheeks. She let her eyelids drop. Her sister Dinarzad exclaimed about how exciting this tale was. Shah Rayar expected this. It had become routine. He looked at the quiet face of his bride. "Your tales overflow with injustice." Scheherazade wanted to say, "Naturally." Instead, she kept her eyes closed.

"The culprit in your stories is always an unreasonable jinni. Do you know nothing of human injustice?"

"Ah," breathed Scheherazade. She wanted to say, "The carpenter's door is falling apart," just as her mother said when people couldn't see their own faults. Instead, she whispered, "I do."

Shah Rayar didn't see the irony in his question. But the girl's answer worried him. Did she guess what his first wife had done? No one should know his shame. But, of course, everyone probably did. After all, why else would he have slain the queen and her servants? He swallowed the painful lump in his throat. The past was behind. The future would be better.

No other wife could serve him so poorly. Still, perhaps he should visit this bride on and off during the day. To check. She would never get the opportunity to betray him that way. Besides, she was nice to look at. ✳

THE TALE OF
KING YUNAN & SAGE DUBAN

"Wake, Sister. Speak, please," called Dinarzad. "Finish your astonishing tale." On cue, like the best trained monkey, Scheherazade continued the tale of the fisherman and the jinni. But the king's morning question had nestled in her brain all day. How could it not? Twice during the day Shah Rayar had dropped by her chambers, that question always burning in his eyes. So she used that very question to shape the next tale.

The fisherman knelt and performed his early evening prayers. His empty stomach clenched. His heart was heavy, for he knew his family waited at home hungrier than ever. Still, he wanted the jinni to understand why he couldn't set him free. Even a jinni deserved that small consideration.

So he sat beside the jar that held the jinni and leaned against it. "Listen, jinni, to the tale of King Yunan and Sage Duban. Listen and understand."

~

KING YUNAN OF PERSIA HAD LEPROSY OF THE MOST VICIOUS SORT. He tried every cure to no avail. Indeed, he was sick and tired of drinking potions and smearing on ointments and submitting to poultices that were as ineffectual as mud.

One day a sage called Duban came to King Yunan's kingdom.

Sage Duban was learned in wisdom from all the great civilizations: Byzantine—which was his own culture—but also Greek, Turkish, Hebrew, Syriac, and, most important for medicinal cures, Arab. He promised to cure the king without any of those supposed remedies that had failed him in the past.

King Yunan liked this sage; he liked him very much.

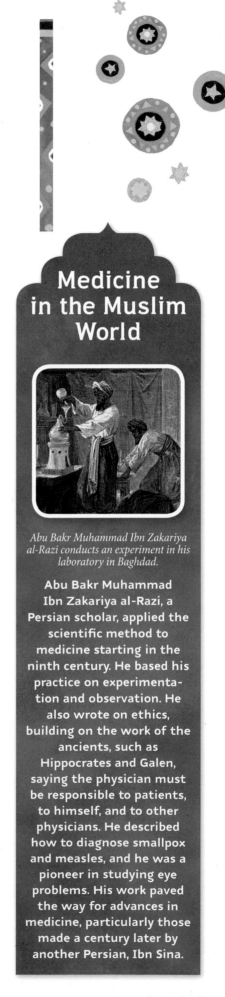

Medicine in the Muslim World

Abu Bakr Muhammad Ibn Zakariya al-Razi conducts an experiment in his laboratory in Baghdad.

Abu Bakr Muhammad Ibn Zakariya al-Razi, a Persian scholar, applied the scientific method to medicine starting in the ninth century. He based his practice on experimentation and observation. He also wrote on ethics, building on the work of the ancients, such as Hippocrates and Galen, saying the physician must be responsible to patients, to himself, and to other physicians. He described how to diagnose smallpox and measles, and he was a pioneer in studying eye problems. His work paved the way for advances in medicine, particularly those made a century later by another Persian, Ibn Sina.

So Sage Duban made a ball and mallet for polo. He hollowed the mallet and its handle, and filled them with drugs that he concocted himself. The next day he advised the king to mount his horse and play polo with that mallet. The idea was that as the king perspired, the drugs in the mallet would seep through the skin of his hands and spread inside his whole body. When he was thoroughly medicated, he should bathe—and just like that, he'd be cured.

It all happened just as Sage Duban promised. King Yunan was so delighted, he invited Sage Duban to sit beside him in the place of honor in the royal hall. The king gave the sage wonderful flowing robes, one trimmed with red fox fur, the other fringed in ostrich feathers. He spent his day talking with the sage, laughing, sharing confidences. It was marvelous to have strong, smooth skin again. Looking in a mirror made King Yunan delirious. No one in the world was wiser than Sage Duban.

All this attention to the sage, however, caused envy in the king's grand vizier. The vizier felt he'd been replaced. He fumed. So he went to the king and decried Sage Duban as an enemy, fixed on robbing the king. "Kill the perfidious sage. Now, before it's too late."

"The ugly snake head of envy has risen in you," said King Yunan. "Sage Duban is a treasured friend. Remember the story of King Sindbad? An envious man urged the king to kill his own son. But the king's vizier told him, 'Don't do what you will regret.' No truer words were ever uttered." King Yunan sighed. "You would have me make a terrible mistake. Just like in the tale of the jealous husband and the parrot."

"I don't know the story of the jealous husband and the parrot," said King Yunan's vizier. "Tell me, please."

Dawn broke and Scheherazade went silent. Her sister Dinarzad spoke her part. Scheherazade repeated her promise of better tales to come. And Shah Rayar agreed to all, as Scheherazade knew he would; this story promised injustice at the hand of humans, not jinn. Scheherazade had been clever enough to live yet one more day. Her fingers curled into fists. She hid them inside her robe. ✳

OPPOSITE: *Sage Duban filled a mallet with drugs. As King Yunan played polo, the drugs seeped through his skin and cured his leprosy. The king loved the sage for this, but the king's vizier hated him.*

31

THE TALES OF THE HUSBAND & THE PARROT & THE OGRESS

"Please begin," said Dinarzad.
Scheherazade complied.

The fisherman cleared his throat, so he could continue his tale about King Yunan and Sage Duban.

～

KING YUNAN, FACED WITH THIS ENVIOUS VIZIER WHO WANTED HIM to kill Sage Duban, told the tale of the husband and the parrot.

～

A jealous man had a beautiful wife. He bought her a talking parrot. Then he left on a journey. When he returned, he asked the parrot what his wife had done in his absence. The parrot told of the wife's escapades with another man. The jealous man exploded in anger and left, vowing not to return for a day.

The wife asked which servant had told on her. The servants pointed to the parrot. So the wife enlisted three maidservants that night. The first maid ground the grinding stone under the parrot's cage. The second sprinkled water over his cage. The third walked past the cage shaking a shining metal plate. They did this all night.

The next day when the husband returned, he asked the parrot what his wife had done the night before. The parrot said, "I couldn't see or hear anything because of the thunder, rain, and lightning." But there had been no storm the night before.

So the husband thought the parrot was a liar—about the storm and about his wife. He killed it.

Only later did he learn from neighbors that the parrot had been loyal. Remorse shrouded him.

The queen's servants fooled the talking parrot into thinking there was a storm all night long. When the parrot told the king about the storm, the king considered him a liar and had him killed.

Talking Birds

A macaw perches on a tree branch.

Talking birds, usually mynahs and parrots, come up in Indian, Persian, Arab, and other tales. Pet birds have been trained to vocalize human speech sounds so well that strangers can understand them. Alex, a famous gray parrot, was studied for over 20 years. He sometimes said things that made sense in a given context. Still, no birds appear to carry on true conversations with humans. What birds communicate to one another through birdsong and other behaviors, however, has yet to be fully understood.

KING YUNAN SHOOK HIS HEAD AT HIS VIZIER. "YOU WOULD HAVE ME kill the loyal Sage Duban and be shrouded in remorse, as well."

"No," said the vizier. "I would save you. In fact, if I am wrong, I would want to die, just as in the tale of the disloyal vizier."

"I don't know this tale," said King Yunan. "Tell me."

And so the vizier told this tale.

≈

A PRINCE WENT HUNTING WITH HIS VIZIER. A STRANGE BEAST CROSSED his path and the vizier urged him to chase it. The prince was soon helplessly lost in the forest.

A girl appeared, weeping. "I am princess of a land beyond the Indus River. I fell asleep on my horse and ended on the ground, alone in a strange land."

The prince invited her to ride behind him on his horse. When they came to a crumbling home, the princess said she must answer a call of nature. She disappeared in the ruins.

She was gone too long for her own safety. So the prince followed. He overheard her talking to children. "I've brought you a fat boy to eat," she sang, "a juicy boy, a blubber boy, a yummy boy." The children drooled, bloodthirsty. She was a ferocious ogress!

The prince ran back to his horse. The ogress followed him. "What's the matter?"

"I fear for my life," he said.

"Pray to the Almighty. That's the answer for the pure of heart."

The prince prayed and the ogress left him. He went home and told his father that the vizier had urged him to follow an ogress. The king put the vizier to death.

≈

"YOU SEE," SAID KING YUNAN'S VIZIER, "ONE MUST NOT FOLLOW THE advice of the treacherous. Sage Duban is treacherous. Look how he cured you simply by having you play polo with that mallet. Think how easily he could kill you. Anything might be fatal—a whiff from a hidden vial. Anything! You are at his mercy. And who knows if he has any? You must kill him first."

King Yunan was stunned. And convinced. No one could count on the mercy of others.

He sent for Sage Duban.

≈

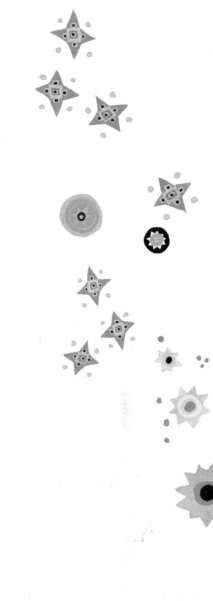

Scheherazade stopped with the morning sun.
Her sister and husband agreed this tale must continue.
Oh, how they wondered what the coming night's tale
would bring. Alas, so did Scheherazade. Her fingertips played
on her lips. Would that they were magic fingers and
could fashion stories from grit, like pearls in oysters. ✸

NIGHT 8

THE TALE OF KING YUNAN
& SAGE DUBAN CONTINUES

"Sister? Tell the tale."
Pearls, thought Scheherazade, let them roll from my lips.

Fisherman," said the jinni, "your tale fascinates me. Let me out of this jar so I can hear better."

The fisherman laughed. "I won't be tricked. Listen."

≈

SAGE DUBAN RUSHED TO THE PALACE AT KING YUNAN'S SUMMONS.

"Today you will die," said King Yunan.

The sage was aghast at the injustice. "Please, King Yunan, if you spare me, the Almighty will reward you. If you destroy me, the Almighty will punish you."

≈

"SAGE DUBAN SAID TO KING YUNAN WHAT I SAID TO YOU," said the fisherman.

"I noticed," said the jinni. "But ..."

"Listen! Let me finish the tale."

≈

THE EXECUTIONER RAISED HIS SWORD.

Sage Duban cried, "Injustice as bad as in the tale of the reward of the crocodile."

"I don't know that story," said King Yunan. "Tell it."

"Not now. I can't think. Let me prepare for death. I'll give alms to the poor and bring back a medical book, full of secrets. If you open it to the sixth leaf, read the third line, and address my severed head, it will answer any question—with knowledge from this world and the other side."

OPPOSITE: *The pages of Sage Duban's book stuck together. King Yunan licked his fingers to try to unstick them. Each lick brought poison to his mouth. So the king died along with the sage.*

When Sage Duban returned, he poured powder on a platter. "Place my head here. Then open this book and ask what you wish."

The executioner sliced off Sage Duban's head. He pressed it onto the powder. Sage Duban's eyes opened. "Now, Your Majesty."

The king opened the book. But the pages were stuck together. He licked his finger to separate them. He licked his finger over and over as he pawed pages. All were blank. The king felt light-headed. He swayed.

"Ah," said Sage Duban. "Listen to my verse."

This king could have grown old and fat.
Instead, he dies pitiless; tit for tat.

The king fell dead from the poison on the pages. Sage Duban's head also died.

"See?" said the fisherman. "When you show mercy, things go better for you."

"I was wrong," said the jinni. "Kindness is the rule, even to those who wrong you. Do not do to me what Imama did to Atika."

"I don't know that tale."

"I can't tell it now. I can hardly breathe," said the jinni. "But I pledge that if you release me, I will do you no harm. To the contrary, I will make you rich."

The fisherman knelt and intoned his evening prayers. The jinni was right: Kindness was the rule. He set the jinni free.

The jinni kicked back into the sea. "Follow me." He led the fisherman over a mountain and to a lake. He told him to cast his net, for he would catch fish in many colors to sell to the king for untold riches. Then the jinni kicked the earth and it swallowed him.

Morning came. And you know very well what Dinarzad and Shah Rayar and Scheherazade did. None of them knew how long this ruse could go on—because by now all three knew it was a ruse.
Wolves toy with shepherds, thought Scheherazade.
Is this husband-king a wolf? But the answer mattered not.
The ruse would go on for at least one more night. One more night, one more dawn, one more hope. ✳

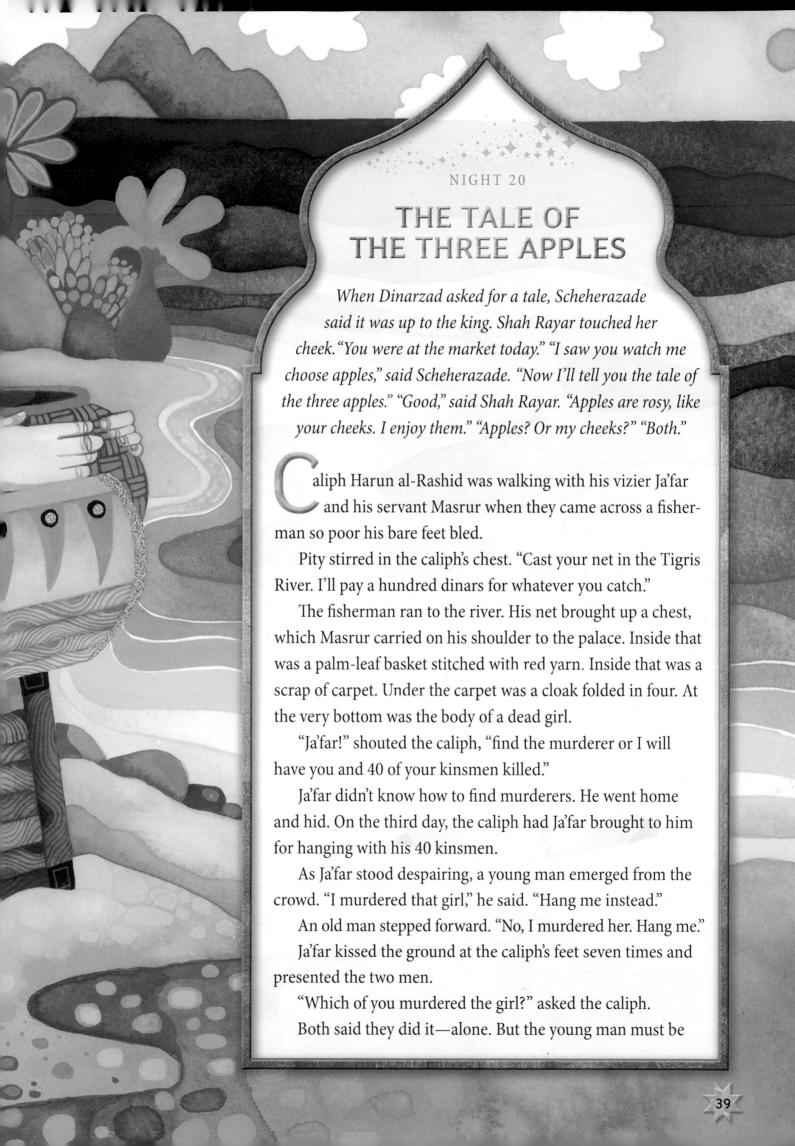

THE TALE OF THE THREE APPLES

When Dinarzad asked for a tale, Scheherazade said it was up to the king. Shah Rayar touched her cheek. "You were at the market today." "I saw you watch me choose apples," said Scheherazade. "Now I'll tell you the tale of the three apples." "Good," said Shah Rayar. "Apples are rosy, like your cheeks. I enjoy them." "Apples? Or my cheeks?" "Both."

Caliph Harun al-Rashid was walking with his vizier Ja'far and his servant Masrur when they came across a fisherman so poor his bare feet bled.

Pity stirred in the caliph's chest. "Cast your net in the Tigris River. I'll pay a hundred dinars for whatever you catch."

The fisherman ran to the river. His net brought up a chest, which Masrur carried on his shoulder to the palace. Inside that was a palm-leaf basket stitched with red yarn. Inside that was a scrap of carpet. Under the carpet was a cloak folded in four. At the very bottom was the body of a dead girl.

"Ja'far!" shouted the caliph, "find the murderer or I will have you and 40 of your kinsmen killed."

Ja'far didn't know how to find murderers. He went home and hid. On the third day, the caliph had Ja'far brought to him for hanging with his 40 kinsmen.

As Ja'far stood despairing, a young man emerged from the crowd. "I murdered that girl," he said. "Hang me instead."

An old man stepped forward. "No, I murdered her. Hang me."

Ja'far kissed the ground at the caliph's feet seven times and presented the two men.

"Which of you murdered the girl?" asked the caliph.

Both said they did it—alone. But the young man must be

PREVIOUS PAGES:

Inside a chest that had been thrown into the sea, the caliph, with his vizier and his servant, found something terrible— a girl's body. Who had killed her? And why?

Political Leaders

A camel caravan stops at an oasis during the Abbasid period.

A caliph is the highest-ranking political officer of an Islamic government. Caliph Harun al-Rashid was a real political leader, ruling Baghdad between 786 and 809. His vizier was Ja'far al-Barmaki. From 750 through the next 300 years, all caliphs were members of the Abbasid family. Like kings, they inherited their political positions. But as Islam spread west across northern Africa and east through Turkey, the Abbasid period—known as the Islamic Golden Age—ended. Various provincial governors and members of ruling families (sultans and amirs) gained importance instead.

guilty, for he knew of the basket, the yarn, the carpet, the cloak—all the details of what was in the chest.

"But why?" asked the caliph. "Tell what happened."

The girl was my wife and the daughter of this old man. She bore me three sons. Then she got gravely ill. One day she craved a bite of apple. But the market had no apples. Nor did the orchards. I had to travel a week to Basra to buy three apples. In my two weeks' absence, my wife had worsened. She couldn't look at apples, much less eat them.

Soon after, a servant passed my shop holding an apple. He told me his lover gave it to him. "Her stupid husband traveled a half month to buy her three."

I rushed home and asked my wife where the three apples were. One was missing! That servant had told the truth! In a rage, I killed her and threw the chest in the Tigris.

When I got home, my son was crying. He'd stolen one of his mother's apples that morning and brought it to market where a servant snatched it. He told the thief how his father had traveled half a month to Basra and back just to fetch that apple and two others for his ailing mother. My son pleaded for the apple. The thief laughed. The boy hid till night, then came home.

"So," said the young man, "I murdered my beloved wife. Hang me."

"No," said the caliph "I will hang the thief. Find him, Ja'far. Or it's you I'll hang."

Ja'far had no idea how to find the thief. He went home and hid again. On the third day, the caliph's messenger came to fetch Ja'far for hanging.

Daylight dawned. "The loyal vizier doesn't deserve to die," said the king. "I must know what happens. Finish the tale in the coming night." Scheherazade would live another day. The east wind bore the fragrance of cloves. Scheherazade had stayed away from her mother these past 20 days to spare her extra pain. But today she would visit and bury her face in her mother's clove-stained hands. For she sorely needed her help. ✳

THE TALE OF
THE VIZIER'S TWO SONS

Scheherazade sipped a special tincture. It smelled like fennel. Her mother had given it to her that afternoon. Women who sipped it didn't bear children. This thought bored a hole in Scheherazade's heart. But what else could she do? If she should be killed while a child grew within her, the child would die, too. That thought bored a hole through her whole self. "Awaken, Scheherazade," called Dinarzad. "Amaze us with a story." Scheherazade dabbed at the corners of her mouth.

The vizier Ja'far made his household members weep for his coming doom. As he hugged his daughter, he felt a bulge in her pouch. It was an apple that their servant, Rayhan, had made her pay two dinars for. Ja'far called for Rayhan. "Where did you get this apple?"

"From a child whose father had brought them from Basra for his sick mother."

Ja'far couldn't believe his luck in finding the culprit. But it was bitter that the culprit was someone he cared for. Still, he took Rayhan to the caliph and explained all.

"What a marvelous coincidence. Your servant caused the death of the woman in the chest." The caliph laughed.

His laughter gave Ja'far an idea. "Let me tell you the tale of the vizier's two sons. If you find it more marvelous, please pardon my servant."

LONG AGO THE KING OF CAIRO'S VIZIER HAD TWO SONS, SHAMS AL-DIN Muhammad and Nur al-Din Ali. When the vizier died, the king appointed his sons as vizier together. Shams al-Din Muhammad was vizier one week; Nur al-Din Ali, the next.

One day, Shams al-Din Muhammad had to leave on a journey. The night before he left he suggested to his brother that they find sisters to marry in a joint wedding. "If our wives conceive on our wedding night, and yours bears a son and mine bears a daughter, let these cousins be married.

"What dowry will you require?" asked Nur al-Din Ali.

"Three thousand dinars, three orchards, three farms."

"You should offer your daughter for nothing!" said Nur al-Din Ali. "Besides, a son is worth more than a daughter."

"A curse upon you!" shouted Shams al-Din Muhammad. "Your frog-faced runt of a son is not worth the clipped-off ends of my daughter's nails after grooming. Not even her toenail clippings!"

In the morning, Nur al-Din Ali filled his saddlebags with gold coins, slung it over his she-mule, added a seat of silk carpet, and crossed the desert. After weeks, he arrived in the port city of Basra.

He happened upon the King of Basra's vizier. The vizier took to him and offered his daughter in marriage. "My brother is a vizier in Egypt," the vizier announced to his friends. "We promised one another our children would marry. This is my brother's son, who has come to marry my daughter."

Nur al-Din Ali gaped. He had not told the old vizier that he was from Egypt nor that he was a son of a vizier. This lie felt remarkably apt to him.

That night the old vizier held a banquet of roasted geese and ox served in silver vessels. The witnesses signed the marriage contract. Spirals of incense rose as the guests left.

Now the old vizier asked Nur al-Din Ali to tell him honestly why he had come to Basra. So the man told his story. The vizier laughed that the brothers had fought over children who didn't exist yet.

Meanwhile, back in Cairo, Shams al-Din Muhammad was having his own adventures.

＝

Morning light dappled the net over the bed. Scheherazade hushed.
Shah Rayar gazed around the room. "I enjoy early hours.
When I was small, I went exploring at dawn, whilst the birds
were still in their nests. Do you enjoy the dawn?"
"The hand in water isn't like the hand in fire," said Scheherazade.
"What does that mean?"
"I enjoy the dawn only once you've said there will be another."
Shah Rayar blinked. Were her words a reproach?
But her face was placid, her tone gentle. "I look forward to
the coming night's tale," he said. ✳

OPPOSITE: *The King of Basra's vizier had a lovely daughter. When the stranger Nur al-Din Ali arrived in town on his donkey, the vizier liked him, so he wed his daughter to him.*

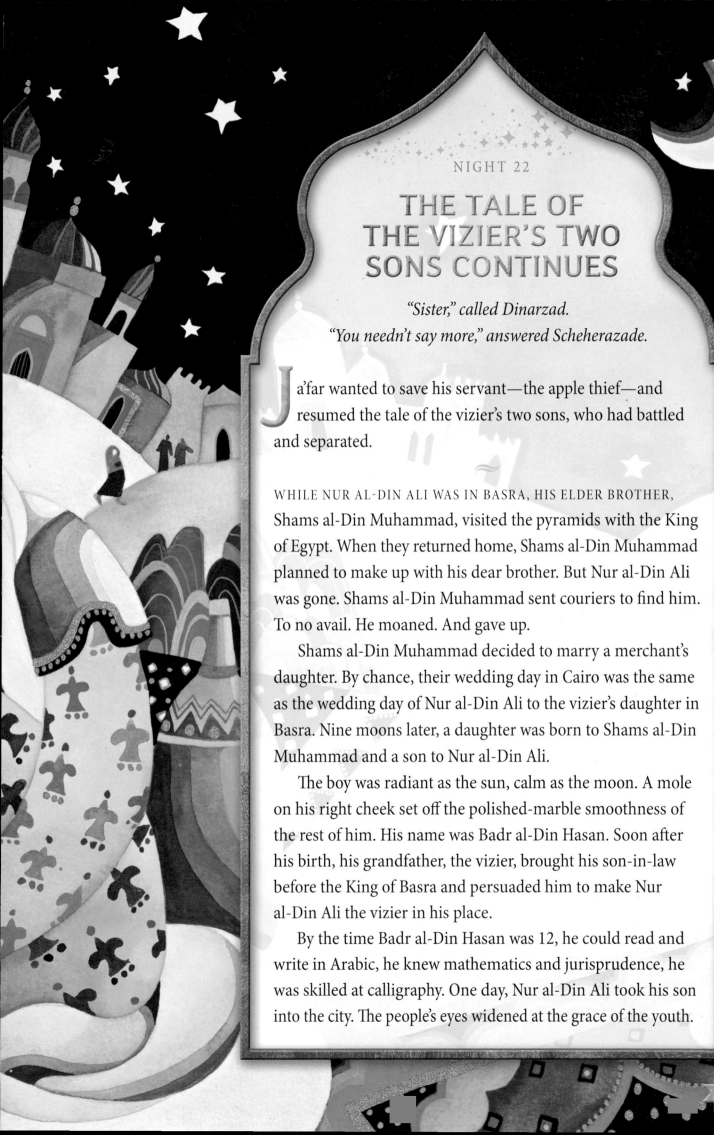

THE TALE OF THE VIZIER'S TWO SONS CONTINUES

"Sister," called Dinarzad.
"You needn't say more," answered Scheherazade.

Ja'far wanted to save his servant—the apple thief—and resumed the tale of the vizier's two sons, who had battled and separated.

WHILE NUR AL-DIN ALI WAS IN BASRA, HIS ELDER BROTHER, Shams al-Din Muhammad, visited the pyramids with the King of Egypt. When they returned home, Shams al-Din Muhammad planned to make up with his dear brother. But Nur al-Din Ali was gone. Shams al-Din Muhammad sent couriers to find him. To no avail. He moaned. And gave up.

Shams al-Din Muhammad decided to marry a merchant's daughter. By chance, their wedding day in Cairo was the same as the wedding day of Nur al-Din Ali to the vizier's daughter in Basra. Nine moons later, a daughter was born to Shams al-Din Muhammad and a son to Nur al-Din Ali.

The boy was radiant as the sun, calm as the moon. A mole on his right cheek set off the polished-marble smoothness of the rest of him. His name was Badr al-Din Hasan. Soon after his birth, his grandfather, the vizier, brought his son-in-law before the King of Basra and persuaded him to make Nur al-Din Ali the vizier in his place.

By the time Badr al-Din Hasan was 12, he could read and write in Arabic, he knew mathematics and jurisprudence, he was skilled at calligraphy. One day, Nur al-Din Ali took his son into the city. The people's eyes widened at the grace of the youth.

PREVIOUS PAGES:
Badr al-Din Hasan's father gave him a scroll that told the story of his leaving Egypt and coming to Basra. The boy sewed it into his turban to keep it safe.

His speech was honey; his smile put the sun to shame. After that, father and son went together everywhere, for Nur al-Din Ali felt himself growing feeble. He had to prepare his son to become vizier.

As the years passed, Nur al-Din Ali missed Egypt and his big brother more and more. One day, he sat down and wept. He told his son of his uncle, the vizier in Egypt. Then he wrote down the story of his departure from Egypt and recorded his wedding date. He rolled up the papyrus and told his son to keep this scroll. Badr al-Din Hasan, who was now 20 years old, sewed the scroll into the skullcap of his turban for safekeeping.

By this time Nur al-Din Ali writhed with the pains of imminent death. "Son, listen well. I have five pieces of advice for you.

"First, live alone. None can be trusted.

"Second, be good to all, or you will incur evil.

"Third, speak rarely, so you don't rue your words.

"Fourth, avoid wine. It will lead you astray.

"Fifth, protect your wealth. It is your safety."

The vizier died. For two cycles of the moon Badr al-Din Hasan mourned his father.

Meanwhile, the king was without a vizier. He wanted Badr al-Din Hasan's counsel. When the young man didn't come to him, he appointed another as vizier, and in a fit of anger he ordered his envoys to seize Badr al-Din Hasan's belongings and lock him out of his home.

But a man raced to warn Badr al-Din Hasan. In the chaos of the moment, the young man covered his head with his robe and ran to visit his father's tomb. On the way there he met a merchant, traveling to the city.

~

Scheherazade sighed with the morning light and fell back into the pillows. "Tell more in the coming night," begged Dinarzad.
"Yes," said Shah Rayar. "Nur al-Din Ali gave his son good advice.
I must know if he will follow it now that he has so much trouble."
Good advice? Did the king truly believe you should trust no one?
Scheherazade had put her trust in her sister, and her life
continued because of that. What a sad man was this king.
Against her will, Scheherazade felt sorry for him.
He needed to learn to trust. And he needed to laugh.
He needed both very badly. ✳

THE TALE OF THE VIZIER'S TWO SONS CONTINUES

"Sister?" *"Hmmm,"* said Scheherazade.
"Wife?" *"Yes,"* said Scheherazade.

J a'far saw that the caliph was enthralled. Maybe he really could save his servant. He continued the tale.

WHEN BADR AL-DIN HASAN TOLD THE MERCHANT HIS NAME, THE merchant was amazed. He had known the youth's father. And he knew that the father's merchant ship was soon coming loaded with goods. He gave the youth a thousand dinars for those goods. Badr al-Din Hasan put the dinars in the purse hanging from his belt. Then he slept on his father's tomb.

The jinniya of that cemetery saw him and was smitten. "Feast your eyes," she said to a jinni as she showed him the sleeping youth.

"He is handsome," said the jinni. "But in Cairo I saw a girl whose loveliness makes the stars, moon, and sun drip with envy. She's daughter of vizier Shams al-Din Muhammad. The king wanted to marry her. But the vizier had just learned that his brother had died in Basra, leaving behind a son—and the girl was betrothed to him."

"What a lunatic," said the jinniya. "Who turns down a king?"

"Indeed. Outraged, the king ordered the girl to marry a cockroach of a man. And the poor girl is the most magnificent human ever."

"No," said the jinniya. "This youth is more magnificent."

"Well, then he's the husband for her. Let's bring him to her fast." The two jinn carried the youth to Cairo, and set him on a bench.

Badr al-Din Hasan woke and looked around bewildered. The jinni bid him go the bathhouse. A man there was preparing for marriage. He should join the wedding procession. If anyone from the bride's procession approached him, he should reach into his purse, where he would find gold coins, and give out handfuls.

Badr al-Din Hasan threw gold coins into the singing women's

Bathing Through the Ages

The Arab baths at Reales Alcázares in Seville, Spain

The earliest public baths date back 4,000 to 5,000 years, to a civilization in the Indus Valley—now Afghanistan and Pakistan. Many cultures have had public baths since, sometimes simply for bathing, but sometimes for social or religious activities. In medieval Japan baths were housed in Buddhist temples and were part of a ritual of purification. In this tale the groom bathes as part of a Muslim cleansing ritual before marriage.

tambourines. The procession went to the home of the vizier, who was the youth's uncle, unbeknownst to them. At the door, the guards turned away strangers, but the singing women insisted the youth who had given them gold be admitted.

Badr al-Din Hasan sat at the groom's right. The groom picked his nose, scratched his buttocks, spit everywhere, and scowled. In contrast, the youth had a gentle, curious smile.

The women played tambourines and flutes as the bride entered. Her braids looped over pearled pouches perfumed with cardamom, ambergris, sandalwood. Birds with ruby eyes, green beryl feet, and golden bills decorated her robe. At her throat hung round blue gems. Yet all that glitter couldn't detract from her eyes, liquid and innocent.

Badr al-Din Hasan swam in those eyes and nearly drowned.

The girl entered the hall fearful. She prayed that the one known as the cockroach had a good heart. But now she saw a youth that looked so much like her he could be taken for her brother. He looked back at her with a hunger that made her blush. Could that be the groom?

The girl dropped her veil. She stood before the youth and nearly wished to die. This was not the groom, for no one would call him a cockroach. Her groom must be the nose-picker beside him.

The guests departed. The groom said to Badr al-Din Hasan, "Leave, stranger. The night belongs to the bride and me."

Badr al-Din Hasan walked away. The jinni stopped him. "Wait here," he said. "When the groom goes to the privy, hurry into the bedchamber. Tell the bride you are her true husband."

≈

The twittering of a white wagtail announced the coming day.
"Tell more in the coming night," said Shah Rayar.
Scheherazade rolled to her side and faced the king.
Her fingers played along the pillow fringe.
"What do you think? Should the youth trust the jinn?"
"He must! That girl is his cousin. They're betrothed."
"But what about his father's first piece of advice?" Scheherazade
feigned confusion. "He said, 'Live alone. None can be trusted.'"
"Now and then, we must trust. The trick is in knowing when and who,"
Shah Rayar replied.
Good, thought Scheherazade. Now to get the king to laugh. ✳

THE TALE OF THE VIZIER'S TWO SONS CONTINUES

"Sister? Please continue your tale," said Dinarzad.
"Of course," said Scheherazade

Ja'far knew he must make the end of his tale more stunning than ever. The life of his servant depended on it.

~

YOUNG BADR AL-DIN HASAN STOOD UNCERTAIN. SHOULD HE TRUST THE jinni? If the cockroach was the rightful husband of that girl, going into the bedchamber would be a lasting offense, the sort a man might kill another over.

But then he remembered the girl's eyes. And he remembered something his mother once said: "If you steal, steal a camel." A camel was a man's most valuable belonging. So stealing a camel was the most despicably horrible act. He swallowed the painful lump in his throat. He wanted to be a good person, not a thief, but he felt linked to this girl.

Badr al-Din Hasan kissed the air—for he was now free and alive and he didn't know how much longer he would be. He squared his shoulders and walked into the bedchamber.

In the meantime, the groom sat in the privy doing what people do in privies. "Meow," came a screech from below. The groom jumped to his feet. Out of the privy flew a black cat. "Meoooooooow!" The cat swelled huge, claws merged into hooves, whiskers became muzzle: It was a donkey. "Hee-haw!" "Help!" called the groom.

The donkey swelled and became a buffalo. He put his face to the groom's and said, "Nasty runt! You stole my wife!"

Fear of the Dark

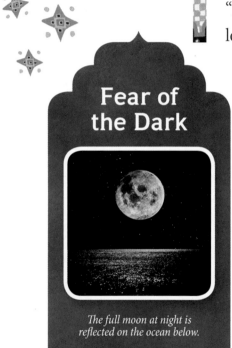

*The full moon at night is
reflected on the ocean below.*

**The two jinn of this tale
fly around at night, but
sleep during the day.
If they are active in day-
time, angels will try to kill
them—as in this story. The
fear of nasty and some-
times mortally dangerous
night creatures is found in
many cultures. Cave paintings from more than 10,000
years ago depict them.
These days many stories
about vampires and other
night monsters sound
foolish, but they may well
have their roots in more
profound ideas about good,
evil, and free will.**

The groom shook his head hard. "The king forced me. I never wanted the vizier's daughter. And no one told me she had a buffalo husband."

"Stay in this privy," said the buffalo, who was really the jinni in disguise. "If you leave, I'll smash you dead. When dawn breaks, then leave. Never come back." The buffalo-jinni picked the groom up and stuck him headfirst into the privy. The groom kicked the air.

All this meant that Badr al-Din Hasan encountered no one when he entered the bedchamber. He lifted the net covering, climbed onto the bed, and waited.

Moments later a small hand lifted the net again. The girl stared. "It's you. I thought someone awful would be here. But it's you. Have I lost my mind? Am I seeing what isn't real?"

"I'm Badr al-Din Hasan. I'm real. What's your name?"

"Sitt al-Husn."

"You're my wife," said Badr al-Din Hasan. Then he said what the jinni had told him to add: "The king paid that other man to pretend to marry you as a joke."

"I didn't find it funny." She shook her head and her curls swayed. "But now I guess I do." She laughed.

Badr al-Din Hasan took off his belt, from which hung the purse with the thousand dinars that the merchant had paid him. He tucked it under the mattress. He took off his turban and skullcap, inside which was sewn his father's message, and put them under the mattress, too. Then he patted the bed beside him. "Shall we get to know one another?"

Afterward, the newlyweds fell asleep, cuddled together.

The two jinn now entered the room. "We must return the youth to the cemetery before he's found in this bedchamber and put to death," said the jinniya. They lifted Badr al-Din Hasan and flew across the desert. But soon the first call to prayer rang out and an angel of the Almighty hurled a star at them. The jinni went up in flames. He died instantly. The jinniya managed to carry Badr al-Din Hasan to the city right below—the city of Damascus—but she didn't dare stay with him since the angels had targeted her.

Badr al-Din Hasan lay at the city gates, wearing nothing but his shirt. People gathered, thinking he must be a drunkard, though a handsome one with a fine shirt. Their gossip woke him. Badr al-Din Hasan asked where he was.

Someone answered, "Don't you know? Where did you fall asleep last night?"

"Cairo," said Badr al-Din Hasan.

"Drunk, indeed! You can't fall asleep in Cairo and wind up awake in Damascus. It's many days' journey in between."

"But it's true," said Badr al-Din Hasan. "Yesterday morning I was in Basra. Last night in Cairo. This morning in Damascus."

"He's not drunk, he's insane. Let's lock him up."

Badr al-Din Hasan ran from the crowd. He went to the first open shop, a cook's shop. It happened that this cook had once been a frightful robber. That was behind him now, but still people feared him. So no one followed Badr al-Din Hasan into the shop.

"What's this all about?" asked the cook. He listened to the whole story and raised an eyebrow. "Surely the Almighty has plans for you. I'll adopt you as my son and protect you."

Meanwhile, the vizier of Egypt, Shams al-Din Muhammad, went into the bedchamber to find his daughter. "Alas, dear Sitt al-Husn. How dreadful your night must have been."

"Dreadful? My night was delightful."

"You call a night with that wretch delightful?"

"Don't joke anymore, Father. You know I spent the night with the beautiful stranger. He must have gone off to the privy now."

Shams al-Din Muhammad ran to the privy and found the groom facedown in the toilet. He pulled him out. "What happened?"

"You're all crazy!" shouted the groom. "Don't you know your daughter's married to a buffalo?"

Shams al-Din Muhammad went back to his daughter's bed-chamber and found the skullcap with the message sewn inside it, the one his brother had written before he died, and he realized that Badr al-Din Hasan was his nephew. Then he found the 1,000 dinars in the purse and he assumed this was the dowry. Ah, he must now find the youth and welcome him home. But that turned out to be harder than he ever could have imagined.

For the next 10 years, Badr al-Din Hasan lived far from his cousin-wife and from the son that was born nine months after the

wedding. Many things happened before Shams al-Din Muhammad finally found his nephew and brought him back to Cairo. Poor Badr al-Din Hasan didn't know that this was his uncle bringing him home—instead, he thought he was a prisoner. Shams al-Din Muhammad told his daughter Sitt al-Husn to go into her bedchamber and when her long-lost husband should enter, she should greet him as though nothing had happened. Then Shams al-Din Muhammad sent Badr al-Din Hasan into the bedchamber of his cousin-wife.

Badr al-Din Hasan finally recognized where he was. This was his wife in front of him. How did it all happen?

His wife, Sitt al-Husn, smiled. "That was rather long in the privy."

"And that," said Ja'far, "is the tale of the vizier's two sons."

"Packed with coincidence," said the caliph.

"More coincidence than this event with the apples and the dead woman we found in the chest in the Tigris. Yes?" Ja'far looked at the caliph with hope.

His servant hugged himself tight and waited.

"Yes," said the caliph. "Your servant can live."

A rooster crowed at sunrise. Scheherazade
closed her mouth. "Marvelous," said Dinarzad.
"What is still hidden is more than what has been revealed,"
said Scheherazade. "Please tell us in the coming night," said Dinarzad.
"If it pleases the king." Shah Rayar was watching Scheherazade
with a strange look on his face. His lips quivered.
Then he smiled. "Don't you know your daughter's married
to a buffalo?" he asked in a mimic of the cockroach groom.
He grinned. "That was rather long in the privy."
And he fell backward laughing. Scheherazade laughed, too.
She had started out telling tales to save the people,
and look how many girls' lives she'd already saved by
staying alive. But maybe her tales could do other things,
as well. She looked at her laughing husband.
Maybe her tales could save a soul. ✳

THE TALE OF QAMAR AL-ZAMAN

"Sister? Tell a tale," begged Dinarzad.
"Willingly," said Scheherazade.

A king called Shah Riman wanted to see his son married before he died. He imagined an elaborate wedding and told his son, Qamar al-Zaman, who was but 15, about it.

Qamar al-Zaman, gentle and dutiful as well as a stunning gift to the eye, shook his head. "I won't marry. I've heard of women's treachery."

Shah Riman felt the world go dark. But he adored his son, so he waited two years before he repeated his request. Qamar al-Zaman fell to his knees. "The Almighty demands obedience from a son. And my affection presses me to obey. But, alas, I will not marry." He recited famous poetry about wily wives and afflicted husbands.

Baffled, Shah Riman consulted his vizier. The vizier stroked his long beard. "Wait a year. Then gather the amirs and soldiers. He cannot disobey in their presence."

A year later, Shah Riman gathered friends and summoned his son, who kissed the ground at his father's feet three times, then stood.

"It is time to wed."

The young man hung his head. Not again. Was his father getting feeble-brained? And look how he'd filled the room with witnesses to coerce a yes. Unfair tactics!

"Never will I marry!"

Shah Riman's heart burst. Everyone was watching; the shame was unbearable. He shouted, "Seize him!"

The king's mamluks, his warriors, dragged Qamar al-Zaman to a tower. The flagstone floor and crumbling walls were dank.

Beauty & Piety

A Muslim woman in Malaysia

In these tales, beautiful creatures are often presented as desirable and ugly creatures as horrible. This focus on external looks and emphasis on beauty was common in the medieval world, not just in the Middle East, but throughout Europe, and in many other times and places from the ancient world to today. Perhaps traditional notions of beauty were connected to ideas of health; that is, if you looked good and smelled good (with the help of perfume), maybe you were healthy—a reproductive and survival benefit.

treasure. The more suitors she rejected, the more suitors came.

King al-Ghayur pressed his daughter to marry. In anger, Princess Budur said, "Entreat me no further, or I will throw myself upon a sword." The king drew back, aghast. Did she actually mean that? He closed her away in a room with 10 duennas—elderly ladies—as guards. King al-Ghayur announced that his daughter had gone mad and needed seclusion.

"That is where Princess Budur, the most beautiful human in the world, abides now," said Dahnash. "At night I gaze on her loveliness."

"Lovely, perhaps," said Maimuna, "but she is not the most beautiful human. I have gazed upon the one who owns that title, earlier tonight."

The jinn argued the point. In the end, they agreed that the only way to settle the debate was to see the youth and the princess side by side. They flew to the far China island and carried Princess Budur, so weary from prisoner-melancholy that she never woke. They lay her beside the youth and compared them from every angle. The jinni thought the girl more beautiful; the jinniya, the youth. Finally, Maimuna slapped the ground and out sprang a one-eyed, scabby, twisted jinni. Pus ran from his ears. Rats peeked from his beard. He drooled. "Qashqash, be judge. Which of these humans is more beautiful?"

Qashqash danced in his hobbley-gobbley way. "You must wake each in turn while the other sleeps, and see if one falls madly in love with the other. The one who does is, by logic, the less beautiful."

The rising sun formed a halo around Shah Rayar, on his side looking at Scheherazade. His eyes were pools of warmth, inviting her to bathe in them. Scheherazade ran her fingers along that halo, coming close enough to stir the hair on his neck, shoulder, and arm but never touch his skin. "Who will win?" asked Dinarzad. "You'll learn in the coming night. If it should please the king." "Let's desist with this ritual of questions," said Shah Rayar. "I will announce when the tales have ended. Until then, continue each night, Scheherazade."
Until his announcement, yes—until then, life would go on.
The future fell like wounded soldiers, looking up and waiting, helpless, with only one question on their minds: Would the next face to appear above them be foe or friend? ✳

THE TALE OF QAMAR AL-ZAMAN CONTINUES

"Sister …" "Listen well."

The two jinn had to figure out who was more beautiful, youth or princess, using Qashqash's test. Dahnash transformed into a flea and bit Qamar al-Zaman. The prince woke and slapped at his neck. But Dahnash had already moved to the princess and bitten her, too; differently—this bite put her into a trancelike sleep.

Qamar al-Zaman sat up. A girl was in his bed! With hair as black as his, eyebrows curved in the same way, cheeks round and ruddy as his own. He felt he looked in a mirror that reflected an improved self. Was she real? He reached for her shoulder, but she rolled and her mouth fell open, like a child's. Qamar al-Zaman lowered his face to hers. Her warm breath rustled his cheek down. He was overcome with the sense of her purity. She must be honest, forthright, loving. How he decided all this from only her aspect in sleep is a mystery of love, for the youth was definitely in love. "Awaken, my darling." But Princess Budur couldn't wake from that trance. The prince moved his lips until they were above hers. One perfect kiss—that's all he wanted.

Dahnash jiggled with pleasure. The prince was intoxicated; Dahnash had won!

Qamar al-Zaman came closer … then stopped. No, no stolen kiss. He would do the right thing. In the morning he'd tell his satisfied father that he would marry her. For surely his father had put her here; how else could she have passed the guard? He slipped the girl's ring onto his own finger. Aha! Even their fingers were the same size. Qamar al-Zaman turned his back and slept.

PREVIOUS PAGES:

Qamar al-Zaman tried to wake the girl in his bed, but she slept in a flea-bite trance. He took her ring. Then the youth fell into a trance and Princess Budur awoke. She was instantly smitten.

Protecting the Insane

A princess sits alone, deep in thought about her prince.

In this tale, the prince and the princess are driven to insanity because they have been kept apart. In the earlier tale of Badr al-Din Hasan (Night 23), a crowd thought he was insane and was going to lock him up. They might well have been thinking of a safe place to protect him rather than a prison, however. In many places the mentally ill were cast out of society, even as recently as a century ago. But the Muslim world was tolerant; therapy was needed, not banishment. As early as the ninth century, Baghdad and Cairo had hospital facilities for the mentally ill.

"See?" said the jinniya Maimuna. "Passion had no hold on him. Let's see if your princess can behave as well." She became a flea and bit Princess Budur on the belly. And, of course, she bit the youth, but with an entrancing bite.

Princess Budur's eyes flew open. A man lay beside her! She drew back in alarm. But he didn't move. She dared to lean across him to see his face. His face was soft—or at least it looked soft; she didn't touch it. She had never touched a youth's face before. The more she studied it, the more she noticed details. Curved lines cupped his mouth; he must laugh a lot. Even closed, his eyes seemed to hold generosity of spirit.

Princess Budur touched her own throat. This was no bully. This was a sensitive soul. Good heavens, she was in love. "Wake," said the princess.

"Come live with me and be my love." Qamar al-Zaman slept on. "Do you spurn me?" The princess took the youth's hand. And still Qamar al-Zaman slept on. "What is this? You took my ring. Oh! That's an act of love if any there is. I shall do the same." She put Qamar al-Zaman's ring on. Then she wrapped her arms around him and slept.

*Scheherazade rubbed her eyes at the dawn light.
"With her arms wrapping him, the story is neatly wrapped up,"
said Shah Rayar. He knit his brows. "You make it seem simple.
The prince had a belief, yet he let love sweep him off
his feet. You make him a fool."
"What about the princess?" said Scheherazade. "She had a belief
and let love sweep her off her feet."
"But her belief was wrong. Not all men want to rule their wives."
"Might it be that not all women betray their husbands?"
"Perhaps. But it could never be so simple,
not like in your story." The nugget of ice in the center
of Scheherazade's chest—that nugget that never melted—
doubled in size. A straightforward love story
could never hold this man's attention.
"The story is not yet ended," said Scheherazade.
"And it is not simple, my husband."*

THE TALE OF QAMAR AL-ZAMAN CONTINUES

*"Sister?" came the eager voice. "Wife?" came the
curious voice. "Patience," said Scheherazade. "Let me fluff
my pillow first." Ah, how good she had become at
bluffing. How many skills of deception would she master
before she died? "Where were we?" she asked nonchalantly.
"Oh, yes. The youth and girl were in love."*

The princess is hugging my youth," said Maimuna. "I won.
But I'll be generous, Dahnash. You can go on living anyway."
Dahnash and Qashqash carried the sleeping princess back to
her home in China.

In the morning when Prince Qamar al-Zaman woke, he searched
around, then called in the mamluk. "What happened to the girl in my
bed last night?"

"No girl was in your bed last night."

"Don't lie!" They quarreled. Qamar al-Zaman grew wild at the growing
fear that the maiden might be withheld from him for good. He slapped
the mamluk's ears, then bashed his head on the floor and, finally, dunked
him headfirst in the well. "I'll drown you if you don't tell the truth."

Spluttering in terror, the mamluk cried, "I will. But first let me go
take off these soaking clothes and put on fresh ones."

"Go," said the prince. "Hurry back!"

Meanwhile, the vizier was advising the distraught king to leave his
son in the tower prison for a moon, to break his spirit. Certainly the
youth would then agree to get married.

The mamluk burst in, dripping water and bleeding from his forehead.
"Disaster!" He described what happened. "The prince has gone mad."

"You stupid, worthless vizier," said the king. "Look how badly things
have gone. Go to the tower and fix this."

The vizier found Qamar al-Zaman reciting the Koran. "What
happened?" asked the vizier, and he told what the mamluk had said.

When Qamar al-Zaman saw that the vizier, too, pretended to know
nothing about the girl, he grabbed him by that long beard and dragged

him—bumping across flagstones, smashing against walls. "Tell me," he said with each marching step. "Tell me, tell me, tell me about that girl."

"I will," cried the vizier. "Let go!" The prince dropped the vizier, who rubbed at his bruises. "Let me catch my breath, then we can talk."

"No. It's time for action. Tell my father I will marry this girl he has chosen for me," said the prince. "Immediately."

As soon as the vizier told the king, Shah Riman hurried to the tower. Alas, his most unfortunate son had gone batty. "It's but a dream, my son."

"When you dream of battle, do you wake with a bloodied sword in your hand? Of course not."

Qamar al-Zaman held out his hand. "This is her ring."

Shah Riman examined the ring. "This changes everything. This is a mystery only the Almighty can solve. We must pray constantly."

"The kingdom cannot run without you, Your Majesty," said the vizier. "Shut yourself away with the prince in a pavilion by the sea. Pray. But set aside two days a week for court ceremonials and judgments on the disputes and needs of your subjects."

So Shah Riman and Qamar al-Zaman moved to the pavilion and prayed. And Shah Riman performed his kingly duties twice a week. But no answer came from the Almighty. Moons grew full and waned and grew full again. Qamar al-Zaman couldn't eat or sleep.

He languished, looking ever more like a skeleton.

Light gleamed on Shah Rayar's top teeth.
"You smile," said Scheherazade.
"The story has taken an unexpected turn."
"I told you it wasn't simple."
"I will worry for the prince all day."
"And have you no worries for the princess?"
Shah Rayar touched Scheherazade's lips with a fingertip. "I hadn't thought about her. But now I'm sure you'll give me much to think about regarding this maiden in the coming night's tale."
When would this man ever see the woman's side of it on his own? ✸

OPPOSITE: *Shah Riman and Qamar al-Zaman stayed in a pavilion by the sea and prayed for understanding of the Almighty's plan. But the youth pined for the lost girl—he couldn't sleep or eat.*

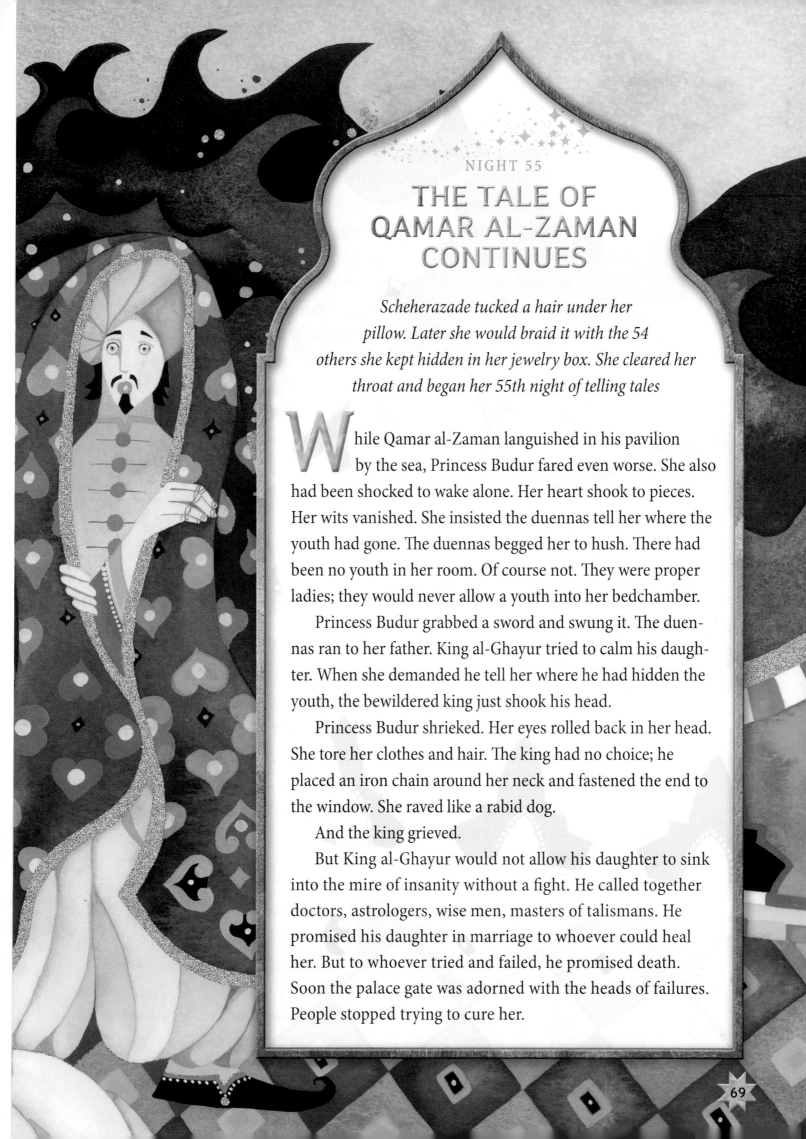

THE TALE OF QAMAR AL-ZAMAN CONTINUES

Scheherazade tucked a hair under her pillow. Later she would braid it with the 54 others she kept hidden in her jewelry box. She cleared her throat and began her 55th night of telling tales

While Qamar al-Zaman languished in his pavilion by the sea, Princess Budur fared even worse. She also had been shocked to wake alone. Her heart shook to pieces. Her wits vanished. She insisted the duennas tell her where the youth had gone. The duennas begged her to hush. There had been no youth in her room. Of course not. They were proper ladies; they would never allow a youth into her bedchamber.

Princess Budur grabbed a sword and swung it. The duennas ran to her father. King al-Ghayur tried to calm his daughter. When she demanded he tell her where he had hidden the youth, the bewildered king just shook his head.

Princess Budur shrieked. Her eyes rolled back in her head. She tore her clothes and hair. The king had no choice; he placed an iron chain around her neck and fastened the end to the window. She raved like a rabid dog.

And the king grieved.

But King al-Ghayur would not allow his daughter to sink into the mire of insanity without a fight. He called together doctors, astrologers, wise men, masters of talismans. He promised his daughter in marriage to whoever could heal her. But to whoever tried and failed, he promised death. Soon the palace gate was adorned with the heads of failures. People stopped trying to cure her.

OPPOSITE:

The princess's foster brother brought the youth to where the princess was locked up. When the princess and the youth were finally reunited, they married immediately. It seemed misery was behind them at last.

Marzuwan realized this must be the Qamar al-Zaman he'd been searching for. Marzuwan walked into the pavilion, straight to the prince. He recited a love poem, and whispered that Princess Budur awaited him, locked in prison in the kingdom of Ghayur. Qamar al-Zaman sat upright. He spoke quietly with Marzuwan, so his father could not hear. They ate and drank. His health quickly returned. Shah Riman had the town celebrate with drums and dancing. The next day Marzuwan planned Qamar al-Zaman's escape, for both knew his father would not allow him to travel yet.

Qamar al-Zaman told his father he was going hunting in the countryside. He filled his saddlebags with money. When they were far from the palace, Qamar al-Zaman and Marzuwan galloped hard. They left behind the servants. After a few days, they killed a camel and a horse, ripped up Qamar al-Zaman's clothes, and threw them in the blood. That way when the king's men found them, they would think the prince had died and give up the search.

They traveled to the islands of King al-Ghayur. Qamar al-Zaman stood in the streets calling, "Scribe, doctor, astrologist, arithmetician—I am all! Who needs my services?"

The townspeople had pity. "Stop your mongering," they warned. "Leave, or your head will wind up on the palace gate, like the head of the other astrologers and arithmeticians."

Qamar al-Zaman didn't stop, of course. King al-Ghayur sent for him. The prince hurried straight to the room where the princess was chained. He stopped outside the curtain and wrote a letter declaring his love. He had the guard deliver it.

Princess Budur unfolded the letter and her own ring dropped into her palm. She read the letter. At last! She planted her feet against the wall and strained until the iron around her neck snapped. She pulled the curtain aside and threw herself into Qamar al-Zaman's arms.

On that day they were wed.

Shah Rayar clapped. "Wonderful tale. All obstacles overcome."
"It's not finished," said Scheherazade. "New obstacles may come."
"What new obstacles?"
"You'll see. The real question is, can they surmount them together?"
"Can they?" asked Shah Rayar.
Scheherazade smiled. ✳

THE TALE OF ALI BABA & THE FORTY THIEVES

"Sister, please continue the last story."

"Of course." Scheherazade finished the story. Then stopped. Silence filled the dark room. Not even the babe made a noise. He had been born a full moon before, the image of his father. Scheherazade's hand traced the features of his face and counted fingers, toes. She kissed him on the top of the head. The silence rippled like a curtain in a breeze. "Sister, won't you start a new story?" How loyal Dinarzad was. Gratitude warmed Scheherazade's chest. She looked into the king's face. It was too dark to see his expression, but moonlight shimmered in his eyes.

"Do you realize, Your Majesty, that I first told you a tale one year ago tonight?" "I was thinking about nothing but that all day," said Shah Rayar. "Your stories mesmerize me. I've figured out why." "Because they make you laugh?"

"Laugh, cry, be astonished. But what holds me fast is that they juggle matters of justice. They reveal how foolish and unfortunate anyone can be." "The unlucky person finds bones in his tripe dinner." "Exactly!" Shah Rayar's hands cupped Scheherazade's cheeks. "You understand that. Tripe has no bones—no one would believe a man who claimed there were bones in his bowl. But you, you understand it. How?" "I follow the light before me. And I pray new lights will continue to come." Shah Rayar sighed. "Your father, my vizier, should name you his heir, so that you become my royal vizier when he dies."

Scheherazade's breath caught. "What? What is it, Wife?"

"My father might not die for years, but I could die any morning." The muscles in Shah Rayar's jaw twitched. His chest ached. For a moment he had forgotten his vow to kill all his wives.

PREVIOUS PAGES:
The cave of the 40 thieves was piled high with all kinds of treasures—carpets, chests, lamps, flasks, bolts of silk. And all of it nestled in a glittering bed of gold coins.

A wife who lived with a man year in and year out was a powerful thing. She could cause a man stinging humiliation. And a wife who gave her husband a plump, hot, wet, squirmy son … Ah, that kind of wife could break a heart. And a wife who told tales that made one see life from a new slant … she could own that heart. Shah Rayar pulled away and crossed his arms at his chest. "Will you begin another tale?" "Yes. But this won't count as tonight's tale; I've already told that. This is extra. Special." "To mark the anniversary?" "To mark your thoughts of this night and the day before it. If your son should cry in the middle, comfort him, for once I begin this tale, you won't want me to stop."

In a town in Persia lived two brothers, Qasim and Ali Baba. They had grown up poor, but Qasim married a rich woman while Ali Baba married a woman poor as sand. Qasim owned a shop and estates, while Ali Baba worked as a woodcutter.

One day when Ali Baba was chopping wood, a dust cloud appeared in the distance. Cautious, he scampered up a tree.

Many men rode up. They tethered the horses and set them to eat barley from sacks hung around their necks. They slung lumpy bags over their shoulders. Ali Baba knew at once they were thieves.

One thief said to a big rock on the hillside, "Open, Sesame." The rock moved aside, like a door. The men entered and the door closed. But they might come out again any second. Ali Baba stayed in the tree and counted their horses. Forty.

The door opened and 40 thieves came out. Their captain said, "Close, Sesame." The door into the hillside closed. The thieves rode off.

Ali Baba approached the rock. "Open, Sesame." The door opened. He stepped inside. Sun lit the cave through a hole in the ceiling. The floor glittered with bales of silk, fine carpets, strange foods. And mountains of gold coins.

Ali Baba took two bags of coins and put them on one of his donkeys. He covered them with wood. He said, "Close, Sesame." The door closed.

Ali Baba drove his donkeys home. He plopped the bags in a circle around his wife.

She heard the clinks as he dropped the bags and shook her head. "Husband, how could you have been so wicked as to steal … ?"

"If you rob a robber, it doesn't count." Ali Baba told her everything.

76

They decided to bury the money until they were sure the thieves had left the area. But first they wanted to know how much it was. So Ali Baba's wife went to Qasim's house to borrow a grain scale.

Qasim's wife was curious. What grain could her in-laws need to weigh? Curiosity pinched her. She dabbed wax on the underside of the scale. Any grain that spilled would stick to the underside.

Ali Baba and his wife weighed the gold. They buried it and the wife returned the scale to Qasim's wife.

Qasim's wife found a gold coin stuck to the bottom. When Qasim came home, she showed him.

Jealousy made bile rise in Qasim's throat. He went to Ali Baba's house. "Brother, why do you act poor and humble when you really have so many gold coins?"

Ali Baba put his hands up as if in surprise. "What are you saying?"

Qasim showed him the coin that had stuck to the scale.

Ali Baba had no choice. He told his brother about the thieves' den. "I'll give you a share if you keep my secret."

"Of course I get a share. But first, where is this cave? How do you get in? Tell, or I'll denounce you to the authorities."

Ali Baba told everything, because, in fact, so much gold was a pleasure that everyone should enjoy. Why not?

Qasim's palms itched till he had to clench his teeth to keep from screaming. The only thing that would satisfy those palms was gold coins. Loads of them. After all, Qasim was important. He deserved money. He put 10 chests on 10 mules and went to the den.

"Open, Sesame!" Qasim entered. "Close, Sesame!" Qasim threw one bag over a shoulder and another bag over the other shoulder and ran to the door. He would fill some chests then he would come back for more.

But Qasim had forgotten the magic word to open the door. "Open, Barley," he said. "Open, Wheat. Open, Rice. Open, Millet." Qasim pulled on his beard. "Open, Chickpeas. Open, Lentils." Qasim paced.

He ran in circles. "Open, Pistachios. Open, Almonds." He put his hands in his hair and shook his scalp.

The sound of hoofbeats came. Qasim was stuck with nowhere to hide in this den. Sweat stung his eyes. He stood right inside the door.

Versatile Wheat

A farmer fills sacks full of recently harvested wheat.

Many grains grow in Middle Eastern countries, and they can be prepared many ways, for different uses and flavors. For example, if you harvest wheat plants when the seeds are soft and yellow (unripe), they can be sun-dried and then set on fire until the husks burn away, leaving the seeds behind. The roasted seeds are rubbed and then cooked. This is firik. Instead, if you let the seeds mature, then you can crush them and have what is called cracked wheat. Or you can boil them briefly and then dry them. This is called bulgur wheat. Or you can dry them and remove the bran (the outer husk) to get the refined wheat that is ground to make pastries.

"Open, Sesame," came the captain's words.

Sesame. Of course. The door opened and Qasim burst out.

The thieves slew him instantly. But how had this man entered the den? No rope hung from the ceiling hole. He must have learned the magic word for the door. What if he had friends who also knew it?

They quartered Qasim's body and put the grisly pieces inside the rock door. That should scare his friends. They rode away to rob again.

When Qasim didn't return home for supper, his wife ran in panic to Ali Baba. "Qasim went to the forest. You can guess why. He hasn't returned."

"Probably he's waiting till midnight so no one sees," said Ali Baba.

Qasim's wife went home, consoled by that logic.

But dread lay heavy on Ali Baba. He hurried with his three donkeys to the den. "Open, Sesame." Alas, poor Qasim! Ali Baba gathered his brother's parts and performed last rites. Then he put the body in two sacks on the back of a donkey and covered all with firewood. He put two bags of coins each on the other two donkeys. He went home.

By now it was dawn, so Ali Baba led the third donkey to his sister-in-law's home. The smart servant Marjana opened the door. Ali Baba told her and the widow the whole sad story. He offered to take his sister-in-law into his home as a second wife, in accord with tradition.

All made a plan to save themselves from the 40 thieves. The widow went to the apothecary shop and asked for a strong medicine. When the apothecary asked who for, she said, "My dear Qasim is ill." The next morning the servant Marjana went to that same apothecary and asked for a stronger medicine. "Poor master," she muttered loud enough for the apothecary to hear. Both days, Ali Baba and his wife rushed back and forth between their home and their sister-in-law's home, as though visiting the ill Qasim. That second night, they set up a lamentation. The neighbors heard and grieved; Qasim was dead.

On the third morning, Marjana visited a cobbler who opened his shop earlier than anyone else. His name was Baba Mustafa. Marjana gave him a gold coin and told him he must walk with her to a fixed point, then she would blindfold him and take him to do a job he must never tell of. She dropped a second coin in his hand.

Once Baba Mustafa was inside the house, Marjana unblindfolded him and asked him to sew together the pieces of Qasim's body. She gave him a third coin. When he finished, she led him blindfolded back

OPPOSITE:

Ali Baba put the pieces of his brother on the back of one donkey, and gold coins on his other donkeys. Then Marjana blindfolded a cobbler and brought him home to sew together the body pieces.

to the fixed point, then she took the blindfold off.

Marjana went home and washed Qasim's body. Ali Baba used incense to cover the rotting odor. He wrapped the corpse in a shroud and performed traditional ceremonies. The carpenter brought the coffin. Marjana paid him at the door, so he couldn't see the body. She and Ali Baba closed Qasim into the coffin and nailed it shut. Neighbors carried the coffin on their shoulders behind the imam, the prayer leader, to the cemetery. Marjana came along, wailing, beating her chest, ripping her hair, as was proper for a servant. Qasim's widow stayed at home weeping with neighbor women, as was proper for a widow.

A few days later, Ali Baba carried his family's belongings to the home of his former sister-in-law, for it was nicer than his old one. The woman was now his second wife. Again, all looked normal. If anyone was watching for an unusual death in town, they wouldn't find it in the death of Qasim.

People were watching, of course. The corpse was absent from their den so the 40 thieves counted the coin sacks. They'd been robbed!

They decided a scout would go into town to listen for talk of a man killed by quartering. That would lead them to the thief, who must die. But if the scout brought back information that didn't lead to the culprit, he'd be put to death.

A volunteer came forward. He entered the town's main square at dawn. The only shop open so early was that of the cobbler Baba Mustafa. The robber scout was surprised. "You're an old fellow to be sewing up shoes. Your eyes must be failing by now."

"My eyes are excellent," said Baba Mustafa. "Recently I sewed together a dead man, inside a house with all the windows closed. Even in the dark I did a superb job."

The scout jumped to attention. "What? Didn't you mean to say you sewed a corpse into his burial shroud?"

"No. I sewed the body together." But now Baba Mustafa remembered his promise of secrecy. "That's all I'll say."

The scout dropped a gold coin in Baba Mustafa's hand. "All I want is to know the house where you did it."

"I was blindfolded for the second part of the path."

"Take me to where they blindfolded you. Then I'll blindfold you and you can see what your feet remember."

He dropped another coin in Baba Mustafa's hand.

They walked to the fixed point. The scout blindfolded the cobbler. Then Baba Mustafa wandered. It was uncanny what his feet remembered. "Here."

The scout took the blindfold off Baba Mustafa. "Who lives here?" But Baba Mustafa didn't know. The scout made a chalk mark on the door and hurried back to the den.

Marjana came out. She saw the chalk mark and sensed it could be there for no good reason. She chalk-marked the neighbors' doors.

Meanwhile, the scout told the 40 thieves all. He led the captain to the street where the cobbler had taken him. There was the chalk mark on the house. The captain pointed to an identical chalk mark on the next house. "Are you sure it's not that house?" The scout was confused now.

They returned to the den, and the first scout offered his neck for execution, as they'd agreed.

A second thief offered himself as scout. He went into town and paid Baba Mustafa to lead him to the culprit's house. He put a mark on the door again, but red this time, and in a less conspicuous place. Marjana saw that red mark. She made red marks on the neighbors' doors. When the captain arrived with the second scout, he didn't know which was the right home of the culprit. The second scout lost his head.

The 40 thieves were now reduced to 38. This had to stop. The captain went into town alone and paid Baba Mustafa to lead him to the culprit's door. He counted the roses on the bush, touched the chip in the third brick under the window, noted the shade of the turquoise in the mosaic over the door.

The captain went back to the den and told the 37 thieves there to scatter to other towns and buy 19 mules and 38 leather oil jars. One of those jars should be brimming with oil; the others, empty. When the men came back, he gave each a knife and had them climb into the empty oil jars. The captain loaded each mule with two jars, and led the procession into town, to Ali Baba's door.

Ali Baba stood in his doorway, enjoying the air after his supper.

"Good fellow, I've traveled far," said the captain, "to sell my oil in the market tomorrow. It's too late to find a public house for the night. Please could I settle here till morning?"

Ali Baba had heard the captain's voice before, but only saying the

Smart Marjana figured out that 37 of the jars held creatures that meant harm to her master. So she poured hot oil into them and killed whoever they held.

words, "Open, Sesame," and "Close, Sesame." He had seen his face, but only from afar. So he didn't recognize him. He welcomed this merchant. They dined and talked of many things.

Finally, Ali Baba asked Marjana to prepare stew for tomorrow, and take good care of the oil merchant. Off he went to bed.

Off went the captain to the courtyard, where the 38 oil jars stood in a row. The captain opened the top of the first jar that held a man, to let in fresh air. He whispered, "When pebbles strike your jar, cut your way out. I'll be waiting." He did likewise to all the jars that held men. Then he went back to the kitchen and Marjana led him to the guest room. He stretched out on the mattress, fully clothed and ready.

Marjana returned to the kitchen and cut up meat for stew. But her lamp went out. There was no more oil in the storeroom. Oh no. The servant Abdullah scoffed at her quandary. She could fill up that lamp with oil from one of the merchant's jars. Marjana took her lamp out to the courtyard. As her footfalls crunched across the pebbles, a man's voice came from the jar nearest her. "Is it time yet?"

Marjana stopped in shock. Whether this was jinni or man, it was mischief. She answered, "Not yet." Each jar she passed asked the same question. She gave the same answer. Until the last jar, which was silent. She opened it, filled her lamp, and hurried back to the kitchen. She carried a large pot out to the last jar and filled it with oil. This she set in the hearth, till the burning oil bubbled. Though Marjana was a good woman, she wouldn't let herself think about what she was about to do. She must protect the household.

She poured boiling oil into the jars from which voices had come to smother whatever soul hid within—fiery or human. Then she turned out her lamp and waited in the kitchen.

The captain soon rose from the bed. He threw pebbles from the window onto the jars. No one came out. His throat tightened. He threw more pebbles. No one stirred. The captain had difficulty swallowing now. He snuck downstairs and went to the first jar. The smell of hot oil assailed his nose. He raced from jar to jar. His men were dead! He climbed over the garden wall and fled.

Marjana went to bed.

In the morning Ali Baba went to the baths. When he returned, Marjana told him what had happened. Ali Baba looked in the jars and saw 37 dead men with knifes in their hands. "But what happened to the oil merchant?"

Marjana was not only cleverer than Ali Baba, she was a master of diplomacy; she didn't call him a dunce. "That was no oil merchant." And she told Ali Baba about the white mark on the door and then the red mark on the door. The thieves had been hunting him.

Ali Baba and the servant Abdullah buried the dead men in secret. Ali Baba hid the jars and knives, and he sent Abdullah with the mules, one by one, to the market to sell.

The captain returned to the den and vowed to get revenge. In the morning he went to the city and took up lodgings there. He brought bolts of silk, brocades, and linens from the den to his lodgings in town. He set up a shop and pretended to be a merchant. His shop was across the way from Qasim's old shop, which was now run by Ali Baba's son. The son was sociable, and soon befriended the new cloth merchant.

The cloth merchant found out that Ali Baba was his new friend's

father. So he invited his friend to supper and gave him carved boxes and quill pens as gifts. Before long, Ali Baba's son felt beholden, but he was poor and didn't know how to repay the merchant's kindness. He asked his father for advice.

Ali Baba told his son to walk with the cloth merchant past Ali Baba's house. Then he would invite them both in for a meal.

The next Friday, when Ali Baba's son and the merchant passed Ali Baba's house, the son said, "This is my father's home. He wants to meet you." He knocked on the door.

The cloth merchant's skin came alive. Finally, he could slay this man.

This was the third time that Ali Baba had encountered the robber captain, but he didn't recognize him. Perhaps his eyes were not so good. "Dear guest, stay for supper."

The merchant said, "I regret I cannot. I don't eat salted food."

"Our bread has no salt. And I'll make sure the stew and meat you get is insipid." Ali Baba went into the kitchen and told Marjana the guest didn't eat salt.

Annoyed, Marjana made a second, saltless, stew. While it cooked, she served the meat. The three men sat on cushions on the floor around an embroidered cloth, as was the custom. Instantly, Marjana recognized the cloth merchant as the robber captain who had come last time posing as an oil merchant. She leaned across him as she set the dishes out. Under the folds of his mantle, she made out the shape of a dagger. Now it all made sense. Any good Persian shares salt with a friend, for salt wards off evil. But this man carried evil in his soul like a favored child.

While Abdullah washed the dishes after the meal, Marjana set up a side table beside Ali Baba on which she placed three cups and a wine flask. "Abdullah and I will now eat our meal, so we won't be of service to you for a while," she said clearly.

The cloth merchant realized this was his opportunity. All he had to do was get Ali Baba and his son drunk. He could stab the father and escape over the garden walls.

But Marjana had a plan, too. She dressed in a long flowing skirt, billowing sleeves, and a headdress that came to a point with a star over the center of her forehead. She wore all gold, the heroic color, and she fiercely hoped she would be the heroine tonight. At her waist

Dancing Hands

An Indian girl performs a traditional dance using her hands to tell a story.

Persian medieval dancers used specific hand shapes, just as dancers in India (which was then called Hindustan) did. In India these hand shapes were called mudras and many gestures had well-defined meanings. In this way, the mudras could tell tales, with details of events as well as emotions. But scholars do not believe the hand shapes in Persia were so precisely linked to particular meanings. Instead, they added to the general tone and feeling of the dance.

was a gilded belt from which hung a dagger in a bejeweled sheath. A thin veil covered from below her eyes to her throat. She handed Abdullah his tambourine and told him to follow her. They went into the eating room and Marjana danced while Abdullah played the tambourine. She glided across the floor, then stood and swayed. Her hands made unusual shapes that evoked sensations of romance and adventure.

Marjana now pulled her dagger out of its sheath. She performed a dance with it, leaping like a gazelle. Finally, she took the tambourine from Abdullah and stretched it out toward Ali Baba, while holding the dagger in her other hand. This was how professional dancers asked for pay. Ali Baba laughed in surprise, but he dropped a coin into the tambourine. Marjana held out that tambourine to Ali Baba's son. The son dropped in a coin. Yes, things were going as she had hoped. Marjana clenched her teeth to hold in fear. She stretched out the tambourine to the robber captain, then plunged the dagger into his heart.

"Dreadful Marjana!" shouted Ali Baba and his son. "You've ruined us!"

"No, I have saved you. Look hard at the face of your enemy."

Ali Baba could see now that it was true. Marjana had saved his life again. "I will wed you to my son, for you have earned the right to be my daughter-in-law."

A warm rush of pleasure filled Ali Baba's son. Marjana was smart, graceful, honest. What more could a man want?

They buried the captain in secret, and the next day Ali Baba's son married Marjana. A year later, Ali Baba visited the den. He took a bag of gold coins and shared the secret of his wealth with his son, who later shared it with his son, who later shared it with his son, and on and on.

Scheherazade had spoken till late morn. She suckled her babe now.

"Wealth forever," said Shah Rayar. "Real life isn't like that, though."

"It could happen in real life," said Scheherazade. "The secret is recognizing the treasure you have and protecting it—using restraint. Then a treasure lasts."

"How did that bumbling man Ali Baba learn restraint?" asked Shah Rayar.

"Do you think Marjana might have played a role? She married the son, so this was her family now—her descendants to protect."

Shah Rayar put a hand on the head of his son and looked thoughtfully at this woman. Would that her tales could reveal all secrets to him.

He kissed her. With restraint. ✸

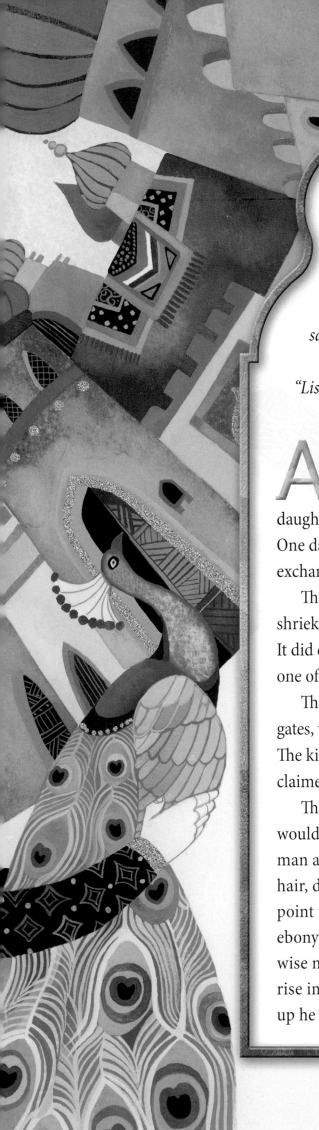

THE TALE OF THE EBONY HORSE

"Sister, the baby has finally quieted down now,"
said Dinarzad. "Could you begin a new story, please?"
"I'll speak very softly," whispered Scheherazade.
"Listen carefully, for this is a new story to begin a new year
of marriage." Shah Rayar moved closer to her.

A king in Persia had three graceful daughters and one brilliant son. Men everywhere wanted to marry his daughters. Women everywhere wanted to marry his son. One day three wise men came to the king, offering gifts in exchange for marriage to his daughters.

The first had a golden peacock that clapped its wings and shrieked at the end of every hour. The king tested the peacock. It did exactly as the man had claimed. So the king gave him one of his daughters in marriage.

The second had a trumpet that, if placed over the city gates, would let out a warning call when an enemy approached. The king tested the trumpet. It also did exactly as the man had claimed. So the king gave him a daughter in marriage, too.

The third had a horse made of ivory and ebony that would take you wherever you wanted to go. The third wise man also happened to be rather nasty to look at, with grimy hair, dirt under his fingernails, and food in his beard. At this point the king's son stepped forward and asked to test the ebony horse. He mounted, but the horse didn't move. The wise man showed him a screw which would make the horse rise into the air. The prince turned the screw and, yes, up he went.

PREVIOUS PAGES:

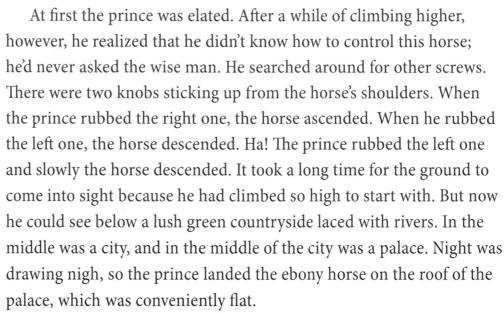

Three wise men offered gifts in exchange for marriage to princesses. One offered a peacock that marked the hours. One offered a trumpet that warned of enemies. And one offered a flying horse.

At first the prince was elated. After a while of climbing higher, however, he realized that he didn't know how to control this horse; he'd never asked the wise man. He searched around for other screws. There were two knobs sticking up from the horse's shoulders. When the prince rubbed the right one, the horse ascended. When he rubbed the left one, the horse descended. Ha! The prince rubbed the left one and slowly the horse descended. It took a long time for the ground to come into sight because he had climbed so high to start with. But now he could see below a lush green countryside laced with rivers. In the middle was a city, and in the middle of the city was a palace. Night was drawing nigh, so the prince landed the ebony horse on the roof of the palace, which was conveniently flat.

The prince left the ebony horse on the roof and climbed down the outer staircase. He found himself in a courtyard paved with marble. He hadn't eaten all day, but he saw no evidence that anyone was awake. There was nothing for him to do but return to the roof hungry and sleep there.

As he was about to climb the stairs again, a light approached. Then voices. It was a group of young women, accompanied by a guard with a sword. In their midst walked a girl who radiated sweetness. The prince stared. A poem entered his head:

> *Twilight's gift, the heart can lift*
> *Beyond the glowing moon, purest pleasure soon.*

The girls stopped in the center of the courtyard and spread out a cloth to sit upon and lit incense to swing about. They talked and played and still the prince watched from the shadows. Then all at once, he stepped forward and knocked over the guard and grabbed his sword.

Dawn showed rosy on the cheek of the babe in Scheherazade's arms. She hushed, and kissed his head on that velvety soft spot that had become her favorite. "You have a knack for stopping at moments that leave me suspended," said Shah Rayar with impatience. Scheherazade smiled. Did he not know that was the point? She kissed her finger then put it to Shah Rayar's lips, and before he could reciprocate, the young mother was asleep. ✸

THE TALE OF THE EBONY HORSE CONTINUES

"I'll hold the baby," said Dinarzad. "Pass him to me, won't you?"
"I can talk with him in my arms," said Scheherazade.
"You've proven that," said Dinarzad. "Pass him for my pleasure."
"Ah, that's different. Of course." Scheherazade settled her son into her
sister's arms. "Now, where was I? Oh yes …"

As the guard fell to the ground at the prince's feet, the young women scattered. All but the one who had caught the prince's eye. "You're my suitor, aren't you?" she said. "Only a spurned suitor would behave so badly. But the king told me you were toady. Instead, you're gallant." She threw her arms around his neck and kissed his cheek. "I will definitely marry you."

"No," said one of the young women, "that's not the suitor your father turned away."

But the princess wouldn't hear their protests. She invited the prince behind a curtain to talk privately.

The princess's attendants revived the fallen guard, who lifted the curtain and asked, "Are you human or jinni?"

"How dare you insult me." The prince brandished the sword. "The king married me to his daughter and sent me here tonight."

The guard backed away, then went shrieking to the king, claiming a jinni had taken his daughter.

The king made haste to the courtyard, sword drawn. He stopped when he found a young man who also held a sword and looked very strong. But the man also looked quite human, clean and well-dressed. So the king sheathed his sword. "What sort of knave are you to pretend to be the son-in-law of me—King of San'a' ?"

"I am a prince from Persia. Do you really think you could find a better match for your daughter than me?"

The king looked the man up and down. "No. But you must ask for her hand in marriage publicly—or the royal family will be shamed."

"I have a better idea. Leave me here tonight. Tomorrow come with your troops and we shall battle. If they kill me, no one will

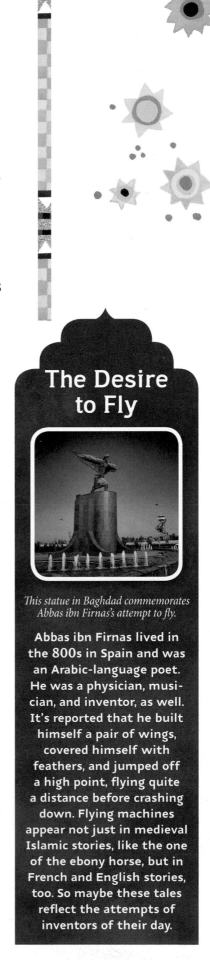

The Desire to Fly

This statue in Baghdad commemorates Abbas ibn Firnas's attempt to fly.

Abbas ibn Firnas lived in the 800s in Spain and was an Arabic-language poet. He was a physician, musician, and inventor, as well. It's reported that he built himself a pair of wings, covered himself with feathers, and jumped off a high point, flying quite a distance before crashing down. Flying machines appear not just in medieval Islamic stories, like the one of the ebony horse, but in French and English stories, too. So maybe these tales reflect the attempts of inventors of their day.

OPPOSITE:

The Persian prince spent the night with a princess and was to battle the king's troops to prove he was worthy of being her husband. Instead, he climbed on the ebony horse and flew away.

know I was with the princess, so your honor will be preserved. If I kill them, I will have earned the title of son-in-law."

This prince's proposal didn't really make sense, but the king accepted it. At dawn he sent for his troops and told the prince to mount a horse to prepare for battle. The prince said he'd wait to see this army first. Soon many soldiers on horseback rode up. "Ack," said the prince. "It's not fair if I'm on foot and they're on horseback."

"What? I told you to mount."

"I'll mount only my own horse. It's on your palace roof."

The king scratched his head. This prince was showing signs of being addled. But the king sent a messenger to fetch the horse, anyway. An army officer went with him. The two of them laughed when they saw the mechanical ebony horse. They carried it to the courtyard.

"You'll see how splendidly it performs," said the prince. "Tell your men to step back the distance an arrow can fly. Then I'll charge them."

The king now figured he was humoring a madman. He had his troops step back.

The prince mounted the ebony horse, and turned the screw. The horse rose into the air and the prince flew off.

*Scheherazade tapped the edge of the bed and Dinarzad
passed the baby up to her. The first ray of sunlight played in
the fuzz on the baby's head. Scheherazade breathed in
his sweetness and settled into the pillows, all energy spent.
"The poor princess," said Dinarzad. "The prince abandoned her."
"If she'd had the chance, she'd have abandoned him," said Shah Rayar.
"Sister, is that true? Is that the sort of girl this princess is?"
But Scheherazade had heard quite enough. She pretended to be asleep.
And she didn't have to pretend for long.* *

THE TALE OF THE EBONY HORSE CONTINUES

"Sister?" said Dinarzad.
Scheherazade passed her sleeping son to her sister,
who waited below the bed.

When the king told his daughter her prince had flown away on a mechanical horse, she threw herself around wailing. She swore not to eat or drink until she was reunited with him.

Meanwhile, the prince rode through clouds until he saw his father's palace below and landed the horse there. His father closed him in a teary embrace. "What happened to the wise man who gave us this ebony horse, Father."

"He's in prison, where he belongs, the scoundrel. I thought I'd never see you again."

"Free him! It is a wonderful horse, and I've had a wonderful adventure. I fell in love."

So the wise man was freed. But the king still refused to let his third daughter marry him. After all, a snaggletoothed man with food in his beard and dirt under his nails didn't seem like the best match for his lovely daughter. The wise man fumed at the injustice. But the king was adamant. Further, he told his son not to ride that horse again. The prince, however, missed the princess fiercely. So what did he do? He climbed on that ebony horse and flew off. The king moaned and swore that when the prince returned, he would destroy the horse.

The prince went searching through the palace of San'a' for his princess. When he found her, he led her up to the roof where he climbed on the ebony horse and bade her to

recognized him, however, for he was now skinny and unkempt.

The prince finally arrived at an inn in the land of Rum and sat down for a drink when he overheard traveling merchants discussing the amazing story they had just heard: A wicked man had stolen a girl and flown away with her on an ebony horse, but she had been rescued. The prince questioned them and learned the location of the palace where the princess had been taken. He cleaned himself up and went there. It was nightfall by then, and the guards wouldn't open the gates. Instead, they sat with him outside the prison and shared a meal, while from inside the prison came a high-pitched wailing. The prince could hardly pay attention to these guards, the wailing was so loud.

When the guards learned this traveler was from Persia, they talked about the miserable Persian sorcerer locked in the prison who had stolen a beautiful princess and brought her here. The king had fallen in love with the girl, but she had gone quite mad. She spoke of flying through the air, and ripped at her clothes and hair and moaned the whole day long. The king couldn't find anyone to cure her, so he despaired. And then the stupid prisoner had the gall to wail all the time, claiming none of it was his fault and no one was fair, and he wasn't a sorcerer, just an inventor, all so loudly that the guards couldn't sleep.

The prince didn't sleep either. A plan formed in his head and he was impatient to act it out.

Scheherazade saw dew on the carpet flower in the white porcelain pot on the windowsill. She hushed.
Shah Rayar smiled at her. He kissed her, then kissed the babe. ✳

OPPOSITE:
The prince heard traveling merchants talk of a princess and a flying horse. He went to the place the princess had been taken to and talked with the guards. And all the while, the inventor of the flying horse wailed from his prison cell.

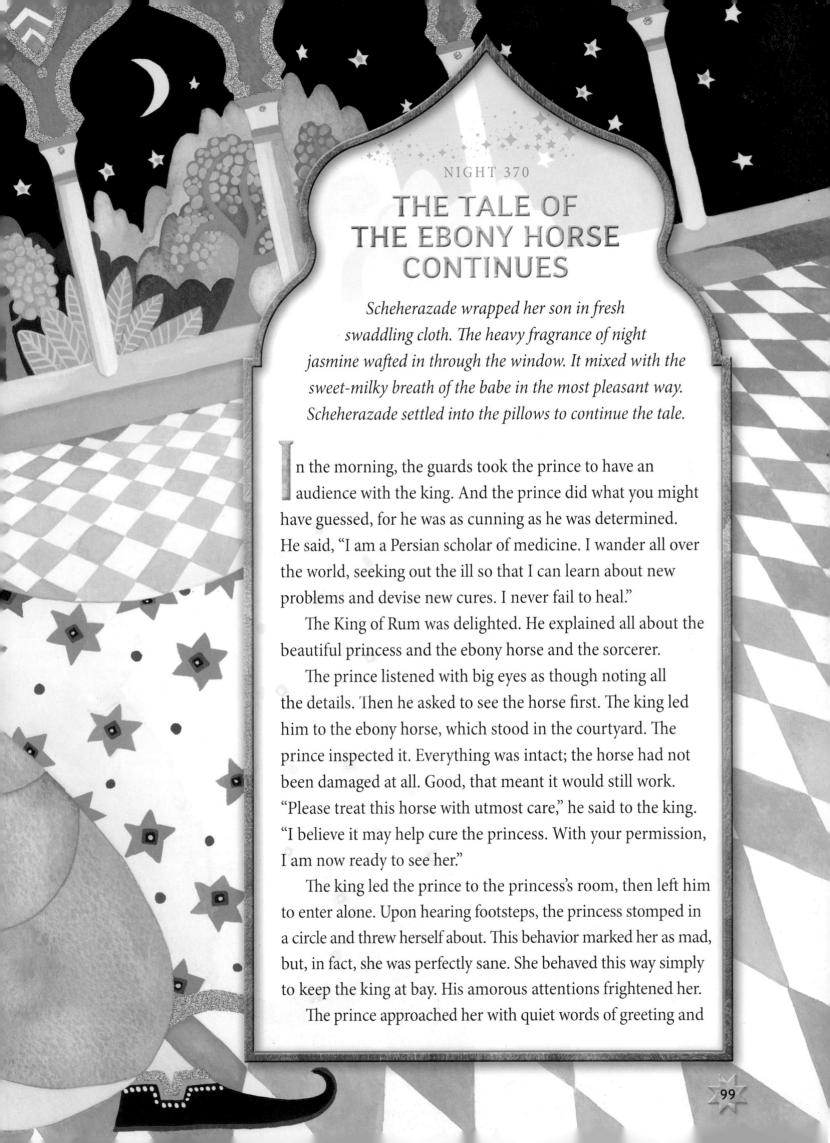

THE TALE OF THE EBONY HORSE CONTINUES

Scheherazade wrapped her son in fresh swaddling cloth. The heavy fragrance of night jasmine wafted in through the window. It mixed with the sweet-milky breath of the babe in the most pleasant way. Scheherazade settled into the pillows to continue the tale.

In the morning, the guards took the prince to have an audience with the king. And the prince did what you might have guessed, for he was as cunning as he was determined. He said, "I am a Persian scholar of medicine. I wander all over the world, seeking out the ill so that I can learn about new problems and devise new cures. I never fail to heal."

The King of Rum was delighted. He explained all about the beautiful princess and the ebony horse and the sorcerer.

The prince listened with big eyes as though noting all the details. Then he asked to see the horse first. The king led him to the ebony horse, which stood in the courtyard. The prince inspected it. Everything was intact; the horse had not been damaged at all. Good, that meant it would still work. "Please treat this horse with utmost care," he said to the king. "I believe it may help cure the princess. With your permission, I am now ready to see her."

The king led the prince to the princess's room, then left him to enter alone. Upon hearing footsteps, the princess stomped in a circle and threw herself about. This behavior marked her as mad, but, in fact, she was perfectly sane. She behaved this way simply to keep the king at bay. His amorous attentions frightened her.

The prince approached her with quiet words of greeting and

PREVIOUS PAGES:

The prince pretended to be a scholar of medicine and went to cure the princess. When she recognized this man as the prince she loved, she fainted from joy.

OPPOSITE:

The princess was as good at deception as the prince. She stood sweetly beside the King of Rum and watched as her prince prepared the flying horse to whisk them both away.

a plea to look at him but not to speak. She looked at him, then looked again. With a shriek of joy, she fainted. The prince rushed to her and cradled her head in his lap. As she came to, he whispered in her ear, "Hush, my love. Don't give us away or we'll both die. I will tell the king I have cured you of your madness, not completely—but close to completely—and that you will obey him. So when he comes to you, act sweet. Trust that I will whisk us away from here. Do you understand?" She nodded.

The prince held the princess close. She seemed fragile and small. He wanted to kiss her, but the risk of someone entering was too great. "Soon," he murmured into her hair. "Soon you will be safe. With me."

The prince left and hurried to the king. "I have treated the girl. She is mending well. If you visit her now and treat her kindly, if you take off her fetters and promise her to grant her every wish, then you will have what you want from her."

The king entered the princess's room. Then he stopped short and waited, uncertain what to do next. The princess stood and walked to him. She kissed the ground in front of his feet. She welcomed him with a smile. "At last," said the king, "at last, you are well again. Come," he called to his servants. "Set her free. Take her to the baths. Dress her in the finest robes. Let her choose the jewelry she wants."

When the princess came back from all these ministrations, she was like the fullest moon surrounded by a million twinkling stars. The king gasped in admiration. "You're perfect."

"And you want her to stay perfect, Your Majesty," said the prince. "So we need to call forth the demon that invaded the princess and we must kill it, so that it may not harm her again. Please have your troops carry the ebony horse out to the meadow where you first found it. Warn them to be careful not to damage it. You and the princess should go there, as well. I will follow. The horse will be part of this final cure, as I told you."

Soon they were all assembled in the meadow. The prince said to the king, "Incense and charmed words will lure the demon out and capture him. Then I will mount the horse with the princess behind me. The horse will walk forward. Each hoofbeat will crush the demon. When the horse reaches you, the princess may dismount, completely healed. You and your troops must stand back while the horse moves, so the demon can't infect you.

Men sitting, talking in the courtyard of Jama Masjid in India

In this tale the king believes cures happen in large part through magic talk and charmed words. The belief in the power of words to transform and heal belongs to many religions around the globe. The child's incantation *abracadabra* (which has a history that intrigues many), used to make monsters disappear or wonders appear, has ancient roots. There is nothing intrinsically childish or religious about word-therapy, however. Calming talk, such as the way the prince whispered to the princess, can be healing, while agitating talk can have negative effects. Likewise, inspirational talk and support groups can also be healing. They help people recover from grief and traumas.

And so the king and his troops retreated a good distance, while the prince and the princess mounted the ebony horse and flew away. The king stood looking up into the air for the rest of the day, wondering what had happened. When he finally realized the girl was gone for good, he cried. But his troops said the healer who had taken her was obviously a demon himself, and the king was lucky he hadn't been harmed in this encounter.

When the prince got home, he married the princess. His father, overjoyed at having his son back, demolished the ebony horse so they could never fly off again. The prince wrote to the princess's father, the King of San'a', explaining that they had married and the princess was well. So in the end, everyone was happy. The prince, the princess, and both kings gave thanks to the Almighty.

Dawn came. Scheherazade lapsed into silence.
"But, Sister," said Dinarzad, "what happened to the unwise man?"
"He was in prison in Rum."

"But eventually he'd get out."

"Probably. Still, he was alone, without his precious horse, without the princess. Isn't that enough suffering?"

"I don't understand the princess," said Shah Rayar. "Why did she pretend to be mad rather than demand to be sent home."

"If the King of Rum had transported her home, the prince couldn't have rescued her. It wouldn't have been as good a story."

"Ah. I like rescues. Women need to be rescued."

"Men need to be rescued, too."

Shah Rayar frowned. Then he lifted an eyebrow. "Rescued from jinn, you mean?"

"Rescued from terrible situations."

"Men can rescue themselves from terrible situations."

"Not always."

The king played with the tips of his beard. "I wouldn't enjoy stories about men who couldn't rescue themselves from terrible situations."

Scheherazade recognized the challenge. She bit her tongue and kept silent. She mustn't take the challenge until she was sure she could win. ✷

The King of Rum stared. The girl who was about to marry him was riding off on a flying horse. And the man who had cured her was riding off on that horse, too. What was going on?

THE TALE OF SINDBAD THE SAILOR

Scheherazade had been telling tales of different kinds for months—about poets, servants, simpletons, and kings. She had told about tricks between husbands and wives, and thieves and merchants. Some were funny or silly, some were mysterious or magical. But none were about men in terrible situations who needed rescue. Such stories somehow wouldn't come into her mind. So she peppered the months with stories about animals: wolves, foxes, crows, serpents, mules, parrots. Shah Rayar listened. But he mentioned how the animals were rather ordinary. That made Scheherazade chew on her bottom lip in worry.

She propped her son under her left arm and rubbed her right palm round and round on her increasingly rounded belly. The tiny baby inside seemed to flip from one side to the other as she pushed on him. She imagined him, in the dark, swimming endlessly. What would it be like to swim endlessly without any sense of where you were and who else might be lurking in that dark? Aha! "Are you ready to listen, Husband?"

"You know I am." "I am, too," called Dinarzad from below.

Long ago in Baghdad a porter named Sindbad was paid to carry firewood from the forest to a man's home. He put the wood in a basket and placed the basket on his head and walked and walked. The sun beat down. When he was halfway there, he stopped for a rest on a bench outside a big house. From the open front door came the scents of caraway, basil, tarragon, and rue. Best was the smell of the dark brown liquid that runs off from fermented barley. He breathed it

PREVIOUS PAGES:

Sindbad the Porter, a poor man, was called inside by Sindbad the Sailor, a rich man, to talk about a song the poor man had sung. Both of them believed fortune was fickle.

and nearly swooned. The people inside were having a feast. The porter's mouth watered.

Birdsong wafted out through that door, too. Nightingales, turtledoves, curlews, and thrushes. The porter leaned to the side for a peek, but he couldn't see. He walked to the doorway. A verdant garden lay within. Servants scurried along porticoes at the edges of the garden carrying jugs of wine and platters of meats. The porter rocked side to side on his bench and sang:

> *Some are rich, some are poor.*
> *Some have less, some have more.*
> *Inside, our souls are all the same.*
> *But I have nothing; this man has fame.*
> *Still, the Almighty makes these decisions.*
> *Only a fool would imagine revisions.*

The porter turned to leave, but a servant clasped his hand. "My master beckons you."

The porter quaked. The master must have overheard his verse and been insulted. When he reached the master, he kissed the ground in front of him. But the master bade him sit and eat. Ground lamb with honey and vinegar and so many spices. Hot flatbread. Dried dates steeped in milk. Lentils and turnips flavored with the root galangal. A fish with a roasted head, a baked middle, and a fried tail. The porter ate until he had room for no more.

The master tilted his head and asked his name and job.

"I am Sindbad the Porter. People pay me to carry things on my head."

"Wonderful name!" said the master with a grin. "I am Sindbad the Sailor. Please repeat for me the verses you recited before."

"I was tired, master. I meant no harm. Please don't be harsh."

"Harsh? I enjoyed them. Please, repeat them."

So the porter repeated his verses.

"So true," said Sindbad the Sailor. "The ways of the Almighty confound. I can tell you stories that prove just how fickle is the matter of fortune. I went on seven sea voyages, full of toil and peril. Would you like to hear about them?"

*Morning silenced Scheherazade. "I want to hear about them,"
said Dinarzad. "Me too," said Shah Rayar. "This sailor is as wealthy
as a king." "In the coming night," whispered Scheherazade.
She smiled, yawned, and slept.* ✳

THE TALE OF SINDBAD THE SAILOR, VOYAGE 1

Scheherazade patted her belly and let the words flow.

G ather, friends, as I tell of my first voyage," said Sindbad the
Sailor. To Sindbad the Porter's surprise, the servants gathered.
This man called his servants friends! The porter moved closer.

～

MY FATHER DIED WHEN I WAS SMALL, LEAVING A GRAND INHERITANCE.
When I became a man, I was greedy; I squandered everything
on fancy clothes and high living. Everything except one property.
I sold that. With the money I bought provisions for trading.
I took a job on a ship sailing from the town of Basra.

Ah, the open sea. We sailed from island to island, growing rich.
Each time the ship docked, I ran over the landing plank eager for
adventure.

One day, as I was cooking stew on a small island, shouts came.
"Run!" It was the captain, calling from the ship. "This is no island,"
he yelled as he pulled up anchor. "It's the back of a giant fish.
Winds dropped sand on it, birds dropped seeds, trees grew. When
you lit that cooking fire, the fish got hot. It will dive into deep
waters now. Run!"

Instantly the island sank. Waves crashed over it. We swam after
the ship, but the sails whisked it away. One by one, the cries around
me ceased. A washtub from the ship floated past and I grabbed
hold. The waves carried the tub through the night and just when
I felt I could hold on no more, the tub bumped against a branch. I
climbed onto it and found myself on an island.

I had been there several days when I saw a mare tethered to a
tree. A man came up out of the ground, clasped my hand, and pulled

Unstable Islands

A Marsh Arab settlement near Basra in southern Iraq

Basra is in the southeast of what is now Iraq. It sits on the river Shatt al-Arab, where the two great rivers, the Euphrates and the Tigris, merge. It empties into the Persian Gulf. There are marshlands on both sides of the river, with dozens of islands, many inhabited until recent times. Some "Marsh Arabs" lived on artificial islands made of reeds. They must have been easily destroyed in storms. Perhaps that is the source of the fantastic idea that an "island" could really be the back of a sleeping fish.

me down into an underground vault. He fed me fine food and told me he was a groom of King Mihrajan. Each month the grooms brought mares to the shore and tethered them at intervals, then hid to watch.

I soon learned why. We stayed at the mouth of the vault, our eyes on the mare. Suddenly a huge seahorse emerged from the water and mated with the mare. He bit at the tether so he could take the mare into the sea, but it held firm. The groom burst forth, banging his sword against his buckler. The seahorse plunged back into the sea.

"Our mares' foals will be worth a fortune," said the groom.

Many grooms gathered then, leading pregnant mares. "Come with us," they said. We galloped to the city of King Mihrajan. The king declared that the Almighty had saved me for a good purpose. He put me in charge of port trading. I worked hard and made him wealthier. But homesickness for Baghdad grew within me.

A large ship came into port one day and I traded with the captain. He told me, "We're returning to Basra, so I'll sell you the goods of a sailor who drowned and I'll keep the money for his family, who lives in Baghdad."

My heart beat fast. "What was the man's name?"

"Sindbad the Sailor."

I held him by the shoulders. "My captain! I am Sindbad the Sailor!"

The captain pulled back. "Scoundrel! How dare you claim the goods of a drowned man."

"But I am who I am." I listed my goods in his hull. I described what happened on the ship before it stranded me. The listening crew cheered. I sold my goods, bade the king farewell, and journeyed home via Basra. With my earnings, I built this house.

~

Dawn warmed Scheherazade's cheeks.
"Sindbad the Sailor needed rescue," said Dinarzad.
What a delightful sister, thought Scheherazade.
Shah Rayar's eyes told how much he had enjoyed that adventure.
Scheherazade sighed in relief. ✳

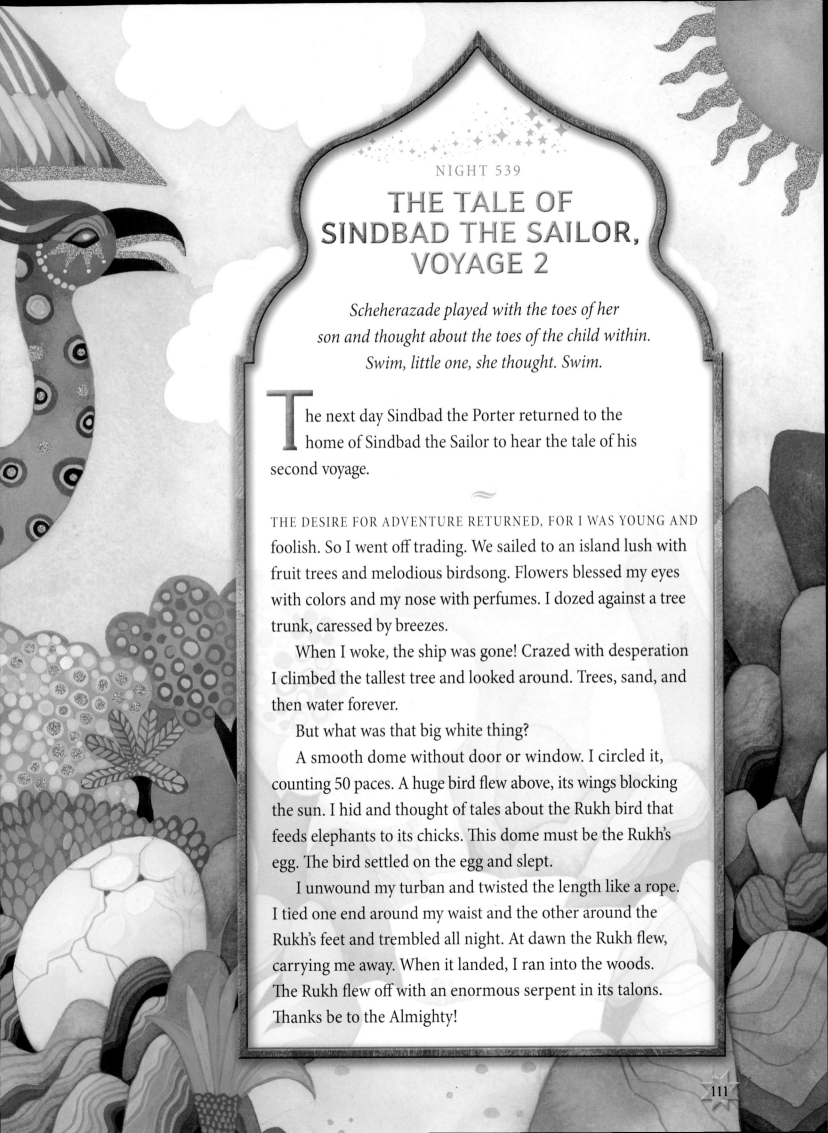

THE TALE OF SINDBAD THE SAILOR, VOYAGE 2

*Scheherazade played with the toes of her
son and thought about the toes of the child within.
Swim, little one, she thought. Swim.*

The next day Sindbad the Porter returned to the home of Sindbad the Sailor to hear the tale of his second voyage.

THE DESIRE FOR ADVENTURE RETURNED, FOR I WAS YOUNG AND foolish. So I went off trading. We sailed to an island lush with fruit trees and melodious birdsong. Flowers blessed my eyes with colors and my nose with perfumes. I dozed against a tree trunk, caressed by breezes.

When I woke, the ship was gone! Crazed with desperation I climbed the tallest tree and looked around. Trees, sand, and then water forever.

But what was that big white thing?

A smooth dome without door or window. I circled it, counting 50 paces. A huge bird flew above, its wings blocking the sun. I hid and thought of tales about the Rukh bird that feeds elephants to its chicks. This dome must be the Rukh's egg. The bird settled on the egg and slept.

I unwound my turban and twisted the length like a rope. I tied one end around my waist and the other around the Rukh's feet and trembled all night. At dawn the Rukh flew, carrying me away. When it landed, I ran into the woods. The Rukh flew off with an enormous serpent in its talons. Thanks be to the Almighty!

PREVIOUS PAGES:

Sindbad the Sailor tied the ends of his untwisted turban around the feet of the gigantic Rukh bird and managed to hitch a ride with the bird, and thus escape.

I walked to a crest. The valley below had no trees or streams. Dazzling diamonds littered the ground. I stuffed many inside my shirt. That evening serpents came out of hiding places. I ducked into a cave and pulled a rock across the front, but when I turned around, an enormous serpent was behind me, curled around eggs. I stared at it all night, sure I was doomed. When dawn came, I stumbled outside.

As I crossed the valley, a slaughtered sheep fell from the sky.

I jumped back, then remembered tales of a land of diamonds so dangerous no one could enter. So diamond hunters cut up sheep and threw meat from the mountaintops. Diamonds embedded in the sheep flesh. Eagles swooped, hooked chunks in their talons, and flew back to the mountaintops. The diamond hunters rushed out at them. They stole the meat with the diamonds.

That must be what was happening now. I picked diamonds from the flesh and stuffed my clothes. Another slab of meat fell right on me. I bound myself to it with my turban rope. An eagle carried it and me to a mountaintop. A man rushed the eagle, screaming. I stood. The diamond hunter cried out in fear and disappointment.

"Don't be afraid," I said. "Don't be disappointed. I will give you diamonds." I told him my tale.

"We will rescue you," said the diamond hunter. Soon other diamond hunters joined us. We ate mutton and slept under stars. In the morning we walked the ridge to an adjoining island full of camphor trees large enough to shade a hundred men. We saw wild cattle and buffalo and a beast called a rhinoceros with a single horn the length of four women head to toe, on which was an elephant. The elephant died and its fat melted in the sun. A Rukh came by and snatched it for its young.

We traveled to Basra. From there I made my way home to Baghdad. I was diamond-wealthy, so I bought presents for friends and furnished my home lavishly.

~

They shared another meal. Sindbad the Sailor gave Sindbad the Porter a hundred gold coins and invited him to return the next day.

Morning sealed Scheherazade's lips. ✴

THE TALE OF
SINDBAD THE SAILOR, VOYAGE 3

*Scheherazade propped pillows around son
and husband, then began.*

Sindbad the Porter returned to the home of Sindbad the Sailor. After eating, everyone belched appreciatively, and the sailor told of the third voyage.

~

THAT URGE FOR NEW MARVELS SNUCK BACK INTO MY HEART, DESPITE my aging body. I hopped on another ship.

One day a wild wind made the sea roar and slap us around till we came to an island. The captain shrieked. "This is the Mountain of the Apes! No one has ever escaped it."

Small, black, hairy apes swarmed the ship. Yellow eyes gleamed as they chewed through ropes, making the sails flap crazily. They threw us off and sailed away.

In the center of the island was a castle with a courtyard, where we slept the rest of that day. At sunset, the earth rumbled. A giant the size of a palm tree lumbered in. His teeth were boar tusks, his blubbery lips flopped against his chest, his eyes burned like torches, his nails curled into lion claws. He picked me up and felt me like a butcher feels a lamb. He dropped me and felt the next man. He went through us all until he reached the fat captain. He snapped his neck, roasted him, and ate him. Then he slept.

We didn't dare move. Morning came and the giant left. We wept and searched for a hiding spot. No caves, no thick forests, nothing! When night fell, we panicked. Who knew what worse monsters lurked here? We returned to the courtyard. Again the earth rumbled and the giant selected a man, ate him, and slept. In the morning he left.

We tore planks of wood from the castle and built a raft. Then we realized that if another ship should stop, the giant would eat more good souls. We had to kill him before leaving.

We returned to the castle. The giant ate another man and fell asleep. We grabbed the iron roasting spits and jammed them into his eyes.

He screamed and searched for us. We dodged each grab. He crashed out of the courtyard, and returned with an enormous giantess. We raced for the raft and floated away, but the giantess hurled boulders, killing all but three of us.

The raft carried us to an island. We jumped off and slept. When we woke, a serpent was curled around us. It swallowed one of us. We heard his bones crack inside the serpent's belly. When it left, we looked for a means of escape. Nothing! That night, the two of us climbed a tree. The serpent slithered up, ate the other man, then left.

I tied pieces of wood around me, as though I was in a coffin. When night came, the serpent tried to swallow me, but the wood made it impossible.

In the morning, praise be to the Almighty, a ship passed. I swung branches over my head and called out. The ship took me aboard. The captain gave me the goods of one of their passengers who had been lost at sea. That passenger's name was Sindbad the Sailor. When I told him that was me, he doubted me. But I told him everything that had happened and described the marks on my bales, and he was convinced.

We sailed to the Indus Valley and I sold my goods at a profit. Along the way I saw a cow that was really a fish! I saw a bird emerge from a seashell floating in the waves and lay its eggs on the cushion of the water!

I returned to Basra and from there to Baghdad. I gave alms to the poor and gifts to friends.

~

Everyone ate again. Sindbad the Sailor gave Sindbad the Porter a hundred gold coins. He begged him to return.

Scheherazade's son's downy hair turned dawn-gold.
"A third rescue," said Dinarzad.
"Each situation more terrible than the last," said Shah Rayar. "But these are stories. Not real lands."
"They feel real to me," said Dinarzad. "Jinn and serpents … such evil exists."
"It's the evil that men do that interests me most," said Shah Rayar.
Scheherazade sighed and twisted the bed cover in her hands. ✹

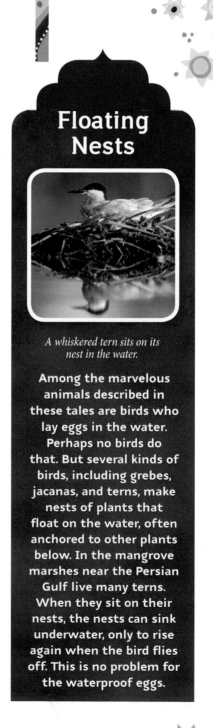

OPPOSITE: *A hideous jinni lived in a castle on the island. He selected the fat captain for doom. He killed him, roasted him, and ate him. The next night he selected the next fattest sailor.*

Floating Nests

A whiskered tern sits on its nest in the water.

Among the marvelous animals described in these tales are birds who lay eggs in the water. Perhaps no birds do that. But several kinds of birds, including grebes, jacanas, and terns, make nests of plants that float on the water, often anchored to other plants below. In the mangrove marshes near the Persian Gulf live many terns. When they sit on their nests, the nests can sink underwater, only to rise again when the bird flies off. This is no problem for the waterproof eggs.

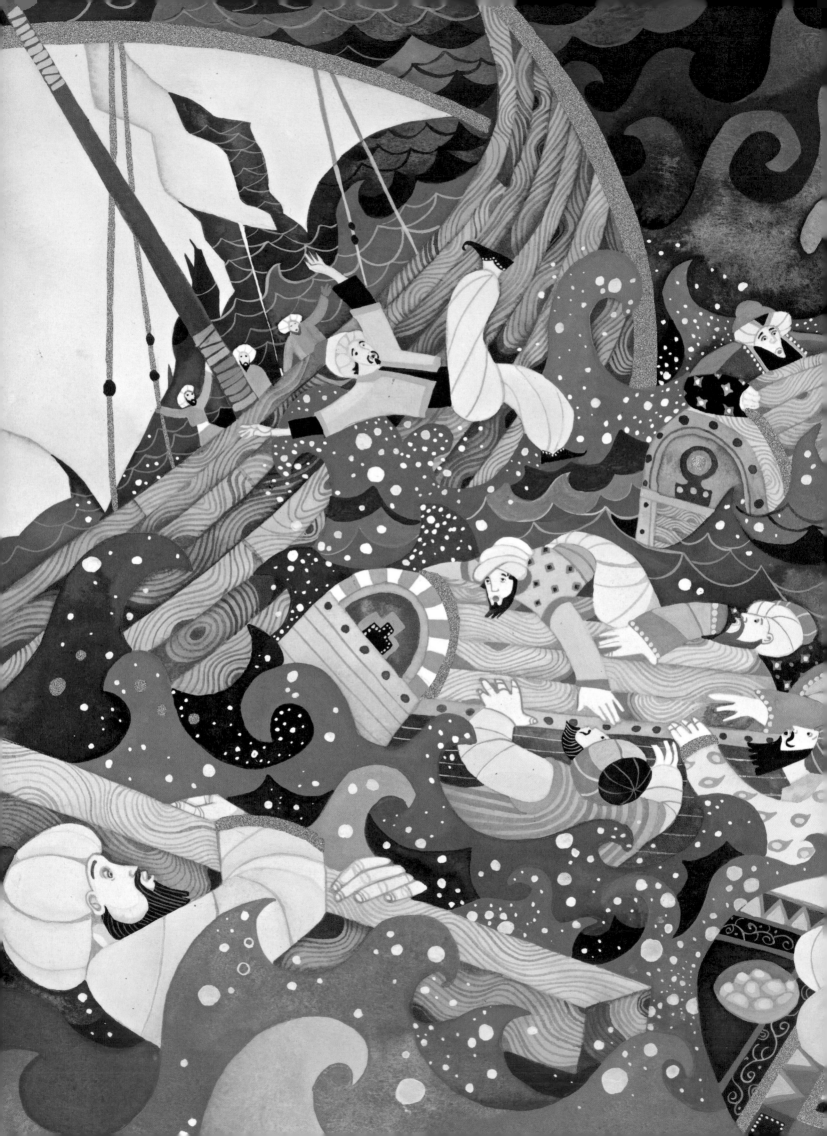

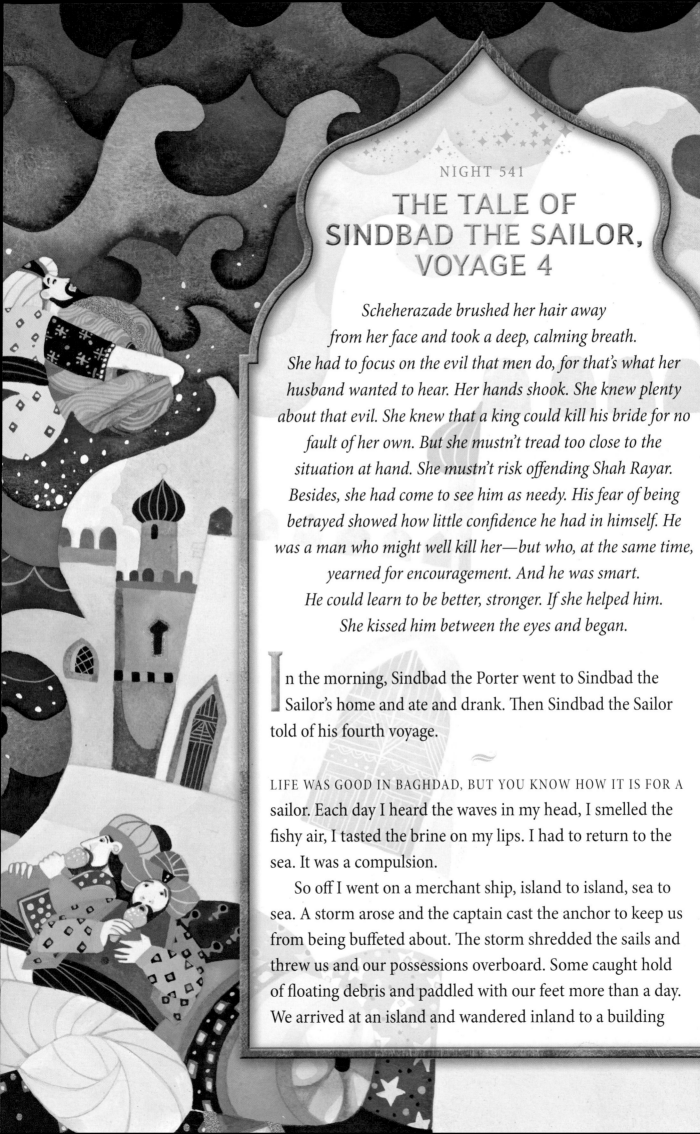

THE TALE OF SINDBAD THE SAILOR, VOYAGE 4

*Scheherazade brushed her hair away
from her face and took a deep, calming breath.
She had to focus on the evil that men do, for that's what her
husband wanted to hear. Her hands shook. She knew plenty
about that evil. She knew that a king could kill his bride for no
fault of her own. But she mustn't tread too close to the
situation at hand. She mustn't risk offending Shah Rayar.
Besides, she had come to see him as needy. His fear of being
betrayed showed how little confidence he had in himself. He
was a man who might well kill her—but who, at the same time,
yearned for encouragement. And he was smart.
He could learn to be better, stronger. If she helped him.
She kissed him between the eyes and began.*

In the morning, Sindbad the Porter went to Sindbad the Sailor's home and ate and drank. Then Sindbad the Sailor told of his fourth voyage.

LIFE WAS GOOD IN BAGHDAD, BUT YOU KNOW HOW IT IS FOR A sailor. Each day I heard the waves in my head, I smelled the fishy air, I tasted the brine on my lips. I had to return to the sea. It was a compulsion.

So off I went on a merchant ship, island to island, sea to sea. A storm arose and the captain cast the anchor to keep us from being buffeted about. The storm shredded the sails and threw us and our possessions overboard. Some caught hold of floating debris and paddled with our feet more than a day. We arrived at an island and wandered inland to a building

PREVIOUS PAGES:

A squall at sea turned into a tempest so powerful and horrific that it destroyed the ship. Those men who could cling to planks and chests paddled to shore.

Horses in History

An Arabian foal and mare run through a field of buttercup flowers.

Humans domesticated horses some 6,000 years ago. We don't know exactly when saddles first appeared, but the cavalry used them in Assyria around 700 B.C. Stirrups didn't show up for maybe another thousand years, when we see evidence of them in China. It wasn't until medieval times, though, that stirrups made their way westward to Europe and the Middle East. Stirrups had an enormous effect on societies because they allowed the rider much more flexibility of movement, including being able to more accurately hunt and fight using handheld weapons.

from which burst fierce men. They dragged us to their king.

The king, however, smiled and fed us strange food, the smell of which turned my stomach. So I held back, even though I was famished, while the others ate. Soon they were reeling and their eyes rolled back in their heads. The fierce men rubbed them with coconut oil so their skin would expand. Day after day they fed them. My fellow sailors grew fat. I wasted away, though, for I remembered the tale of jinn who fattened up humans to eat. But I couldn't dissuade my friends from eating, for the food drugged them silly. Every day a man took them out to pasture, and they ate and ate. They were cattle to these cannibals.

I followed the others out to pasture, wobbling I was so weak. The herder noticed me and saw that my eyes were clear and my ribs showed and he realized I hadn't been drugged. Who knows why, but he took pity on me. He gestured to me to turn back. He pointed the direction I should go. I ran as best I could. I came to a road and followed it.

For an entire week I trudged that road night and day, till I came to a group of men. Amazed at my tale, they fed me and took me in their ship to their home. The king of this new land received me warmly. What a marvelous city it was, with all kinds of food and traders with all kinds of goods. The hustle and bustle made me miss Baghdad. The king and I became friends and one day I asked him why he never used a saddle, but preferred to ride bareback.

"What's a saddle?"

I called a carpenter to fashion a saddle. I made a pad out of wool, covered it with leather, and added straps. I had a blacksmith make stirrups from which I hung silk fringes. The king called it glorious. His vizier wanted one. Other leading men wanted one. I had a thriving business in no time, and I became wealthy and esteemed. The king had me marry a lovely woman—sweet, pretty, and rich. We lived in a large house adjoining the palace. All was right with the world.

One day the wife of a friend died. He wailed, which is suitable, of course, but I told him to be consoled, for the Almighty would present him another wife soon enough. He blinked. "How could that be, when I am to die tomorrow?"

"You are sad, naturally," I said. "But don't exaggerate. Men lose wives all the time. You won't die of this grief."

"But my wife will be buried tomorrow and I will go with her. That is our custom. Husband and wife share life and death."

Could it really be so? The next day I followed the funeral procession to a stone-lined well. They threw in the corpse, in the finest gown with her best jewels. They lowered in my friend, her husband, by a rope tied around his chest, with seven loaves of bread and a jug of water. Once at the bottom, he untied the rope. They hauled it up and covered the well with a giant stone. I imagined him quaking down there, also in his best clothes, with rings on his fingers and bells on his toes. What good would all that finery do him now?

I hugged myself so hard, my fingers dug into my flesh. I asked the king if they treated foreigners like me the same as townsfolk. Indeed, they did. Fear made me walk in circles.

As fate would have it, my own wife soon fell ill and died. I screamed that I didn't share their customs, I wasn't one of them, they shouldn't do this to me. But I found myself lowered down the well after her. I refused to untie the rope from under my arms, so they threw it down upon me. The stone clumped into place. The well went dark.

I felt around. Bones and bodies in different stages of decay littered the cavern floor. The stench nauseated me so badly, I had to crawl. I curled up in a niche in the side of the cave and slowly doled out my pitiful supply of water and bread.

I don't know how long I was like that, perhaps 10 days, perhaps more. I was very careful to eat only when I thought I'd pass out from hunger. I had to make this food and water last till I could find a way to escape. But, alas, it was disappearing. I chewed on my fist to allay hunger. Then I heard the scrape of stone on stone. A shaft of light entered through the well. A dead man came hurtling down. Then a woman was lowered. She untied the rope and it disappeared upward. The stone was set back in place. The light ceased.

The widow cried softly, unaware that I huddled there, listening. And, may the Almighty forgive me, already thinking ahead.

She was doomed. And it was her own fault. She belonged to this country; she believed in this disgusting custom. She deserved to die. She might even look forward to death. But she had with her seven loaves of bread and a jug of water. Why should it go to waste?

Especially when I was there. And I did not deserve to die—I did not believe in their vile custom. I picked up a thick bone and slew her. One blow was all it took.

I curled up in a recess in the wall and doled out my pitiful supply of water and bread. I didn't think about the dead woman. I didn't think about what would come next. Still, a cold rock of knowledge filled my chest. I don't know how many moons I survived in that cavern, killing the spouses of the dead and existing on their meager rations, but it was many.

One day, or perhaps night, since the two were the same to me, I heard rummaging. I stood, and the rummaging turned into a scurrying that quickly receded. I followed it to the other end of the cavern and saw a dim light and the tail of the wild beast as it escaped through a hole. The side of the cavern was at such a slant here, I had to lie on my stomach and shimmy along. Hurrah! The hole was large enough and I was now emaciated enough that I could fit through. But I still had my wits about me. So instead of escaping immediately, I went back and gathered the jewels of the dead and wrapped them in their silk clothes. I left that cavern with bundles of wealth.

I headed for the seashore and waited. A ship came and I waved the white blouse of a dead nobleman over my head. They took me aboard and I told the captain my tale. But I didn't tell him about the well and my time in the cavern. I didn't think he'd understand the choices I'd made. I didn't understand them myself.

I returned to Baghdad via Basra. I fed the poor and clothed the widows and provided for the orphans, for no one understood better than me how harsh life could be.

~

Sindbad the Sailor fell silent. No one spoke. They ate, and Sindbad the Porter collected his hundred gold coins and went home.

Scheherazade fell silent, too.
Rain pattered outside the window. Dawn was gloomy.
No word came from Dinarzad. No word came from Shah Rayar.
The evil that men do had silenced them all. ✳

OPPOSITE:
Sindbad the Sailor escaped through a hole in the mountainside. But before he left, he gathered up all the riches he could carry from the dead bodies inside the cavern.

121

THE TALE OF SINDBAD THE SAILOR, VOYAGE 5

Shah Rayar ran a finger down Scheherazade's chin and neck, to the hollow at the base of her throat. His lips moved, as though he swallowed words. She took his hand and held it tight. This was the moment for stories. He wanted to know about the evil men do, so that's what he'd get.

At the break of dawn, Sindbad the Porter hurried to Sindbad the Sailor's house. Sindbad the Sailor told of his fifth voyage.

MY HEART WAS ADDICTED TO THE SEA. THIS TIME I BOUGHT A ship and hired a captain and crew so I'd never get stranded again. Safety, at last. So I thought.

We visited many countries, then landed on an uninhabited island. The others went exploring. One ran back. "Come see a giant egg. Like a dome!"

A Rukh egg! I raced to the crew, but they had already bashed the egg open.

The sky turned black as Rukh wings blocked out the sun. We ran for the ship. The bird and her mate screamed and circled above. We set sail and the birds flapped toward the island. A moment later they returned with boulders in their talons. The male hurled his. It crashed through the water with such force, we saw the seabed. The female hurled hers. The ship splintered!

I grasped a floating plank and paddled with my feet to an island bursting with fruits and flowers. In the morning I saw an old man squatting beside a spring. He motioned me over

PREVIOUS PAGES:
The sailors had broken a Rukh egg. The grieving parents dropped boulders on the ship in revenge. The ship sank, poor sailors! Sindbad the Sailor paddled away on a plank to an island.

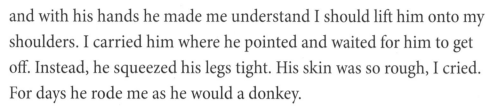

and with his hands he made me understand I should lift him onto my shoulders. I carried him where he pointed and waited for him to get off. Instead, he squeezed his legs tight. His skin was so rough, I cried. For days he rode me as he would a donkey.

One day I found old gourds on the ground. I pressed grapes into one, plugged it, and set it in the sun. Soon the juice fermented into a crude wine. Drinking it relieved my neck and shoulder pain. The old man grabbed it, drank it all, and passed out. I pried his legs loose and set him on the ground. But I knew he would come after me, and I'd be his slave again. So I killed him with a huge rock. I told myself he was a monster, not a human gone astray.

I wandered the island, despondent, when I discovered an anchored ship. I told the passengers my tale. They called the man who had enslaved me the Old Man of the Sea. We traveled to another island, with a big city. Apes lived in the surrounding mountains. At night they came into the city to kill everyone they passed, so the people got into boats and rowed out to sea to sleep. They returned in the morning when the apes went back to the mountains.

I explored the city that day. But when I went to the docks, I found my ship had sailed without me. I shivered, remembering the hateful apes from my third voyage. But a man brought me into his boat to spend the night. The next day he gave me a bag to fill with pebbles and he sent me with his friends into a valley of tall trees. When the apes saw us, they fled up those trees. I don't know why they didn't kill us. We threw pebbles. The apes pulled coconuts off the trees and lobbed them back at us. For many moons I collected coconuts to sell. I became rich.

One day a ship visited. I got on board with a cargo of coconuts. I traded them for pepper and cinnamon with such pungency the birds went dizzy, and Chinese aloewood—which, fresh, gave a perfume and, dry, made good furniture and cooking ware—and, best of all, pearls. By the time I got home, I was richer than ever.

Everyone feasted. Sindbad the Porter ambled home with a hundred gold coins, wondering about the Old Man of the Sea. Was he a monster or just a troublesome old man?

124

The rains of the day before had left puddles in the pits of the windowsills. Dawn glistened there. "I hope the old man was a monster," said Dinarzad. "You can't kill someone for being troublesome." "He was more than troublesome," said Shah Rayar. "He caused pain." "But is pain a reason to end the life of one of the Almighty's creatures?" The question hung in the damp air. ✷

THE TALE OF SINDBAD THE SAILOR, VOYAGE 6

*Shah Rayar took his fussy babe into his arms. The boy quieted.
"You're a charm," whispered Scheherazade.
Shah Rayar's lips brushed her cheek. "You've convinced me."
"That you're charming?"
"That men do evil. Maybe this sailor could show redeeming features?"
"Listen well," said Scheherazade. "Everyone has redeeming features if they submit to the will of the Almighty."*

Sindbad the Porter ran to the home of Sindbad the Sailor, who told of his sixth voyage.

I STILL HADN'T LEARNED MY LESSON, SO I SET OUT ON A MERCHANT SHIP. We entered a sea the captain had not planned to visit. He pulled on his beard, slapped his face, and thrashed on the deck. "Pray!" he shouted, "or we are all lost." He climbed the mast to loosen the sails, but a high wind arose and the rudder broke. The wind pushed us into the side of a craggy island. The crash destroyed the ship. We plunged into the sea.

Many made it to shore. Treasures littered the coastal inlets: the cargoes of wrecked ships. We gathered it and climbed to a high spot and drank from a delicious stream. Pearls and jewels shone from the bottom. It was easy to view most of the island from there. Chinese aloewood grew in abundance. A stream of ambergris flowed straight to the sea, where giant sea beasts drank it, then swam deep before spitting it out to harden and float on the water's surface. Sailors sell those lumps for incense, perfume, and cures

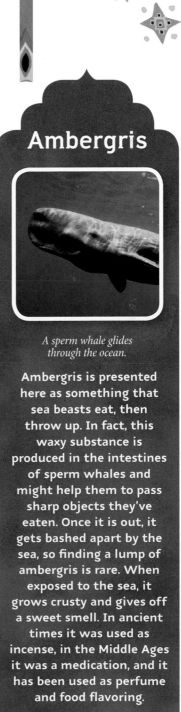

Ambergris

A sperm whale glides through the ocean.

Ambergris is presented here as something that sea beasts eat, then throw up. In fact, this waxy substance is produced in the intestines of sperm whales and might help them to pass sharp objects they've eaten. Once it is out, it gets bashed apart by the sea, so finding a lump of ambergris is rare. When exposed to the sea, it grows crusty and gives off a sweet smell. In ancient times it was used as incense, in the Middle Ages it was a medication, and it has been used as perfume and food flavoring.

for head pain and the shakes. We tried to get to the stream, but it ran through impenetrable parts of a mountain.

We went back to the shore with buckets of sweet water and looked at all we had gathered. Treasures galore, but little food. We grew thin, then emaciated. One man died of starvation. We wrapped him in clothes strewn on the shore and buried him. Each day more died. In the end, I was alone. Hideous! I dug my own grave and lay in it. That way the winds would blow sand over my body and I'd have a burial.

But lying there, I thought about that mountain stream. I picked up a plank of wood from a wrecked ship and climbed the mountain. I lay on the plank and the rushing current carried me down and then straight into the side of a rock face. I hugged the plank tight. The tunnel was so narrow, the plank hit the sides and my head scraped the top. I was sure I would get stuck and die there. I fell into a delirium.

When I woke, the sun nearly blinded me. My plank had docked against land and people stared at me, talking in a strange language. Then one asked in Arabic what I was doing there. I told my tale. They fed me and took me to their king. I had packed along treasures from the shipwrecks, so I gave jewels to this king. We had discussions about my homeland, for his curiosity was great.

One day I learned some people planned a voyage to Baghdad. I bade the king farewell and he gave me gifts for the caliph of Baghdad, since he was impressed with the religious customs of our people. Before leaving he had me tell my tale to his scribes, so they could put it in his library. I traveled home, a happy man.

Sindbad the Sailor grinned. "Eat and return tomorrow for the tale of my final voyage." Sindbad the Porter put his new hundred gold coins in his pouch.

Scheherazade pressed on her belly and the babe within pressed back.
"He's a clever fellow, after all, this sailor," said Shah Rayar.
"But always in need of rescue," said Dinarzad.
"There's no shame in being rescued," mumbled Scheherazade, sleepily.
"Especially when you're clever," said Shah Rayar. ✴

OPPOSITE:
Sindbad the Sailor clung to a plank of wood and was carried by a stream through a mountain and out to the other side. There he found a town with a king who welcomed him.

127

THE TALE OF SINDBAD THE SAILOR, THE FINAL VOYAGE

"Sister, Sister," called Dinarzad, "tell us about the final voyage." "Yes," said Shah Rayar. "Tell us about this clever sailor's seventh and final voyage."

When Sindbad the Porter went to the home of Sindbad the Sailor the next day, he found the meal already prepared and the sailor's servants and neighbors gathered and waiting for his arrival. All ate quickly, then turned to face the sailor, who took a large breath and began the very last tale of the very last voyage.

AFTER ALL OF THESE MISHAPS FROM WHICH I ESCAPED DEATH only due to the great generosity of the Almighty, I should have developed a profound appreciation of the joys of the calm life at home. Indeed, I had. Oh yes. I woke each day knowing I was a lucky man. I breathed in the aromas of my quiet meals and lay back in plump cushions to listen to music and watch dance, and I smiled at all this.

Yet inevitably, the memories of my past adventures faded. That's when I realized I was not yet cured of my desire for travel. Life here in Baghdad was so very known. The unknown out there—out on the sea, out in those jungles, out in those foreign cities—pulled at me till I was wobbly on my feet.

In haste, I put together many possessions, wrapped them in bales, and boarded a merchant ship. Off again. We traveled in high spirits, island to island, ever farther, when one day, on one of the many seas of China, it rained. Steadily. Then drenchingly. We covered our bales with canvas, but still we

PREVIOUS PAGES:

On Sindbad the Sailor's seventh and final voyage, he found himself on a ship that had unwittingly wandered into the farthest sea in the world, full of whales that swallowed sailors.

feared our goods would be ruined and the travel so far would have been for naught. The captain climbed the mast to see if he could spot a good harbor. But then he shrieked and pulled on his beard and slapped his face. Of course, I had seen that kind of behavior before, so I knew it meant the very worst had happened even before he explained that the winds had taken us to the farthest sea in the world and we had little chance of ever returning.

The captain went to his chest of goods. He took out a bag of ashes, wet them and smelled them. Then he opened a small book and read. When he finished, he looked up at us mournfully. "We are doomed. Everyone who enters this region of the sea is swallowed by whales."

At his final word, our ship rose on a swell of sea and we saw a giant whale approaching with a noise like thunder. We cried out. A second whale, even larger and more fearful, appeared from another side. We wept shamelessly. A third whale, the most enormous and hideous of all, appeared from yet another side. We went mad; our death was imminent. They opened their cavernous jaws. In that very moment the ship crashed on a reef and split asunder. I found myself in the turbulent sea, tossed this way and that. When it finally calmed, I swam to a floating plank and attached myself like a tenacious bug and prayed to the Almighty. On each past voyage there had been a point when I realized my folly in traveling and when I regretted having left behind my wonderful home. Never had my regret been greater. "I swear, Almighty One, with all that is good within me, that if you spare me this one last time, I will never travel again. I will never even want to travel again."

That plank floated to an island with freshwater and many fruit trees. I ate and drank and slept. When I woke, I thought of how a stream had carried me to safety on my last voyage. So I managed to fell some of the wonderful sandalwood trees on that island, and to string them together with twine I fashioned from reeds and grasses. I set my raft in the stream and was carried away. The stream was joined by others and soon I was in the center of a raging river. It headed straight for a mountain-side. All the terror I had felt the last time I'd gone on a raft through a mountain tunnel came rushing at me and I tried to veer the raft to the shore. But the current overpowered me, and I found myself once again in a terrible tunnel. This time, though, the stream soon burst out into the open, and carried me through a valley all the way to a bustling city.

The people on the shore threw nets and ropes over my raft and hauled me in to safety. An old man took me home, fed and bathed me, and dressed me in fine silks. For three days I stayed with him, recovering my strength. On the fourth day he suggested we go to market and sell my goods. What goods? I had lost all my possessions when the ship broke on the reef. But I didn't want to contradict this old man after he had been so kind to me. So I said, "As you wish." We went to market and the old man offered my raft for sale—that raft I had made from sandalwood. It turned out that the sandalwood from the forest I had been in was the best quality in the world. No one had seen the likes of it before. The highest bid was a thousand dinars. The old man asked if I wanted to accept that price or if I preferred to wait a while and see if I could get a better price later. I was at a loss, for I had not even realized the raft was valuable. So I said, "As you wish." The old man smiled and offered me a thousand dinars plus an additional hundred dinars if I'd sell the sandalwood to him. "As you wish," I said, for the third time.

We went home and the old man was happy. A few days later he offered me his daughter in marriage. By this point, life felt out of my control entirely. So I answered, "As you wish." We married, and it turned out his daughter was delightful. We fell in love. Soon afterward, the old man died and I inherited his home and belongings. Life was good.

I wandered often among the city people now and I noticed that at the beginning of each cycle of the moon the men grew wings and flew off, leaving the women and children behind. When they returned, life would go on normally until the next cycle of the moon. So I asked a man to carry me with him when he flew off the following time. He refused at first, but I insisted. So at the next cycle of the moon, I climbed on his back without telling my wife or servants, and I flew away with him. We went so high, we were in Heaven itself. I cried out, "Glory be to the Almighty."

At my words, a fire burst from the sky. We barely escaped. The man dropped me on a mountaintop and spluttered many angry words at me and flew off. There I was, alone again and miserable. Two young men appeared from nowhere. They told

Lush Islands

Ripe dates grow on date palm branches.

The islands Sindbad visits are lush with fruits; the seas, full of strange animals. On voyage three he met a jinni "the size of a palm tree" and saw "a cow that was really a fish." The Persian Gulf region has more date palm trees than anywhere else. People eat the fruit and use the wattles and wood to make household goods. The gulf is also home to many unique animals, including the dugong, a marine mammal that can grow up to nine feet (2.7 m) long and grazes on water plants like a cow. There is no real bird similar to the Rukh, however.

OPPOSITE:

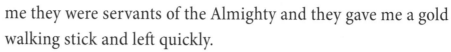

Sindbad the Sailor rode on the back of a flying man who, in fact, was not a follower of the Almighty, but of evil. Sindbad was fortunate the man returned him to his wife.

me they were servants of the Almighty and they gave me a gold walking stick and left quickly.

I walked the ridge of the mountain sure-footed with the aid of the wonderful stick. A serpent appeared with a man flopping out of his mouth, half-swallowed. "Help me," the man cried, "and the Almighty will help you." I smashed that serpent on the head with the gold staff and he spit out the man and left.

The man and I soon came to that man who had flown with me on his back. I apologized for having made him fly so high, since I thought that was what had caused us to almost get burned up. But he told me that it was my words of praise for the Almighty that had nearly caused our doom. He said if I'd hush, he'd carry me home. I got on his back in silence and he flew home with me.

When I told my wife what had happened, she explained that those men were not followers of the Almighty, but of evil, and I must stay away from them. So we sold our possessions, got on a ship, and came back here to Baghdad. We are happy here and I will never travel again. I have no desire for travel. I am finally fully recovered from my obsession.

Sindbad the Sailor crossed his arms on his chest. "What do you think of that, my fine porter?"

"You have earned your wealth," said Sindbad the Porter. "I apologize for having said that wealth was random. The song I sang while I sat on the bench outside your courtyard that first day we met—that song was not true of you."

They feasted. At the end of the day they parted. But ever after Sindbad the Sailor and Sindbad the Porter ate together and talked together often. They were best friends.

Scheherazade hushed with the morning sun.
"Wealth is not random, then," said Shah Rayar.
"Not to those who praise the Almighty," said Dinarzad.
"I like this Sindbad the Sailor. He overcame much."
"And was rescued many times," said Dinarzad.
"Yes. That, too." ✸

THE TALE OF PRINCE HUSSAIN & THE MAGIC CARPET

"Sister? Sister, are you all right?" came the voice of Dinarzad. "Of course. Hush."
"But you groaned in pain." "Don't be silly."
"I heard it, too," said Shah Rayar. "Does your belly hurt?"
"Quiet, both of you. I have a new tale to begin tonight."

The Sultan of the Indies had three sons and one daughter. But the daughter was not his by birth. No, she was his brother's child, orphaned as a tiny babe. So the girl, named Princess Nuronnihar, was the cousin of the three princes, and all were raised together in the palace.

Princess Nuronnihar grew to be an exceedingly charming young woman. She was sweet tempered and had a way with animals. And anyone who looked at her practically swooned, her face was so exquisite.

The princes loved her, as brothers will love a sister. But soon they couldn't help but notice her loveliness. Eyes wide, they watched her dainty ways as she ate. Ears straining, they listened to her lilting melodies as she sang. Noses thrust forward, they followed her as she gathered flowers. Oh yes, they wanted to marry that perfect young lady—all three of them vied for her hand.

The sultan tried hard to get the younger two brothers to yield to the eldest, but they refused. He might have simply declared in favor of the eldest, but that would have left bad feelings. Instead, the sultan made a decree: The princes must go in search of rarities—spectacular, awe-inspiring wonders. The prince who brought back the greatest wonder would get to

*Prince Hussain,
the oldest son of the
Sultan of the Indies,
bought a small,
worn-out carpet as
his choice for what
would be most awe-
inspiring. On it, you
could fly anywhere
in the world in
an instant.*

The Comforts of a Rug

Persian carpets are made with a variety of colors and patterns.

Many cultures produce exquisite traditional rugs, from the land of the Native American Navajo all across the world to China. For nomadic people, in particular, setting up a tent and spreading one's rug on the ground can make an instant home. And if the ground happens to be desert sand, a rug can accommodate unevenness easily. For Muslims, a prayer rug, which can be rolled up to a small size, provides a place for daily prayers, whether they are at home or traveling.

marry the princess. The sultan gave them each a considerably hefty sum of money with which to acquire these rarities.

The brothers took to the road together and stopped at an inn that night. They agreed to part and seek wonders each on his own, but then to meet up again at this same inn in precisely one year, and return home together.

The oldest brother, Prince Hussain, headed toward Bisnagar. Each street of that great city was lined with shops all of the same kind: cloth merchants, flower mongers, craftsmen called out their wares. Linens from India, silks from Persia and China, roses upon roses in garlands for your head or pots for home or shop, and jewels galore. Every merchant wore gold and gems and pearls. They hung from necks, circled arms and fingers and ankles and toes, dangled from the hems of sleeves. And the carpets—the central panels were bordered with mirroring zigzags, floral garlands wove their way throughout like slithering snakes, the grounds were rich red or plunging blue. Each one was different from the others. Prince Hussain imagined taking Princess Nuronnihar to the countryside and spreading out a carpet for them to picnic on, laughing together. Perhaps beside a cool spring. Or beneath a spreading fig tree. He walked from shop to shop, inspecting the underside of each carpet for tight knots, feeling the top for smoothness, asking himself which one might best please his sweet love. They were all wondrous and of top quality, so far as he could see.

Prince Hussain sat down to rest in a shop one day and a passing crier caught his attention, calling out a carpet at a high sum, higher than all the others. Naturally, Prince Hussain was curious. But the carpet was old and worn thin. It was on the small side, though certainly it was large enough for a prayer rug. Still, the merchant declared its virtues. "When you sit on it, it will take you anywhere you wish to go in an instant."

"Anywhere?" asked the prince.

"Anywhere in the world. It flies. Let's sit on it and ride to the room you're staying in."

Prince Hussain took off his shoes and stood barefoot on the carpet. He shivered in anticipation. He sat down on the carpet beside the merchant and wished to be in his room. An instant later, he was. The prince paid the high price happily. Surely he had the rarest wonder of all. He sat on the carpet and wished himself back at the inn, where he waited for his brothers to return.

The middle brother, Prince Ali, had taken the road to Shiraz, the capital of all Persia. That city was known for enchanting gardens, especially its lush fruit trees. It was certain to have just what he needed. He wandered through roses, hunted through orchards. But it wasn't in the splendors of the outdoors that he found his wonder, oh no. It was in the hands of a passing crier: an ivory telescope. The crier asked an exorbitant price. Prince Ali asked a shopkeeper if that crier might be crazy. But the shopkeeper said no; in fact, if the crier was asking a high price, the telescope must have virtues unimagined. The shopkeeper called over the crier, who then boasted that if you looked through the ivory telescope, you could see anything you wanted anywhere in the world. Prince Ali demanded a chance to test the telescope. Joy of joys, he looked through it and saw Princess Nuronnihar laughing with her handmaids. Prince Ali paid the high price instantly, of course. And, after enjoying the pleasures of Shiraz, he returned to the inn, where he found his brother Prince Hussain. Together they awaited their younger brother.

Prince Ali, the second son of the Sultan of the Indies, bought an ivory telescope as his choice for what would be most awe-inspiring. Through it you could see anything anywhere in the world.

The youngest brother, Prince Ahmed, had taken the road to Samarqand. After all, it was a famous city, where merchants from all over came to peddle their wares. He'd be sure to find a fabulous wonder in Samarqand. And very soon, he did. It was an artificial apple, very unassuming in its look. But the crier wanted a huge sum for it. Prince Ahmed leaned forward and sniffed. That artificial apple let off the most pungent smell, as though you were sitting in a bath of stewed apples. The merchant smiled. That smell, that perfume as he called it, could heal anyone of any ailment. Prince Ahmed wanted proof of the artificial apple's virtues, of course. So the merchant called over passing people, and all confirmed that they or their husband or their cousin or their neighbor had been cured of a terrible ill by that very apple. Still, Prince Ahmed wanted to see it in action for himself. So they found a sick man and cured him with the apple. Prince Ahmed paid the high price willingly. Then he set out for the inn to meet his brothers.

Dawn came and brought Scheherazade the comfort of silence. Her back ached. Her legs ached. The baby inside her kicked against her ribs. Now her ribs ached, too. She stifled a groan.

"All three brothers found amazing wonders," said Dinarzad.

"But the carpet is best," said Shah Rayar. "If you fly on a carpet, you can look down on the world with a bird's-eye view. That could give you the advantage in so many things, from trading to warring."

"The telescope can let you see everything, too," said Dinarzad.

"But the carpet can carry you away from danger."

"The artificial apple could heal you if did fall prey to danger."

"But the carpet is best!" Shah Rayar put his heavy hand on Scheherazade's enormous belly. She felt the baby kick at his hand. The king pushed back gently. "Flying is special. The flight of birds can tell you the thoughts of the Almighty."

"The carpet isn't a bird, though."

"No. But the carpet carries you places. It's like Scheherazade's stories. It lets you experience things. I want to experience all that life has to offer."

"Ah," said Dinarzad. "I see now."

Ah, thought Scheherazade. Ah. ✳

THE TALE OF PRINCE HUSSAIN & THE MAGIC CARPET CONTINUES

"Sister? Sister, are you all right?" came the voice of Dinarzad.
"I told you not to ask me that."
"But you groaned. A lot."
"Sometimes people groan when they are expecting a child. Pay attention to the story. Listen." And Scheherazade spoke, haltingly, taking time for deep breaths. There were moments when life started and moments when life ended. Please let this moment be of the first type. She mustered energy for the tale.

The three brother princes met at the inn, as they had agreed. Prince Ahmed showed his artificial apple whose perfume could heal anyone of any ill. He had found it in a town famous for silk things, like carpets. Prince Ali showed his ivory telescope through which you could see anything anywhere. He had bought it in a town that sold the best fruits. And Prince Hussain showed his flying carpet that could carry you anywhere you wanted to go in an instant. He had bought it in a town overflowing with inventions. Each linked to the other; Prince Ahmed, by all reason, should have found the wondrous artificial fruit in the town Prince Ali visited (the one famous for fruits) and Prince Ali should have found the wondrous telescope in the town Prince Hussain had visited (the one famous for inventions) and Prince Hussain should have found the wondrous carpet in the town Prince Ahmed visited (the one famous for silky things). The brothers noticed this fact. Their wondrous finds made a circle, a woven ring, with a united strength that none of them guessed at yet, but all of them sensed.

PREVIOUS PAGES:

The three brother princes compared their findings and realized that the flying carpet, the all-seeing telescope, and the healing apple had to be connected somehow. They were right, as we shall see.

All of them were also impatient to see Princess Nuronnihar again. So it was natural for them to decide to look through that ivory telescope.

Alas! Their beloved princess had taken ill. Doctors couldn't cure her. She wasn't eating, wasn't sleeping. She was in constant pain. Death hovered at her door.

The brothers jumped on the flying carpet. An instant later they were beside the princess's bed. Prince Ahmed held the artificial apple under Princess Nuronnihar's nose. Let it cure her, the brothers pleaded inside their heads. She breathed only shallowly—but, oh, the Almighty is generous, indeed; those shallow breaths were enough. Color returned to Princess Nuronnihar's cheeks. She sat up and smiled—wanly, yes, but genuinely. Her cousin-brothers had saved her—together, by the united strength of their wondrous findings.

The sultan admitted his sons had brought back wonders beyond imagination. But he couldn't choose which was the most wondrous,

since, in fact, it was the coordination of all three together that had saved the princess's life. And it never occurred to him to ask the princess if she had a preference, either for a particular gift or a particular prince. The sultan was not very smart that way, you see. So the dim-witted sultan made a new decree. The princes would shoot arrows; the one whose arrow went the farthest would win the princess.

Prince Hussain shot first. Then came Prince Ali, and he shot farther. Then came Prince Ahmed. His arrow flew out of sight. The sultan declared him disqualified, since no one could find the arrow, which meant it was impossible to measure how far it had gone. So Prince Ali won.

Prince Hussain spluttered and choked. Everything had gone wrong. Princess Nuronnihar was the love of his life. This was too much to bear. He ceded his right to inherit the crown to his brother Ali and he left, to lead the hermit life of a deeply religious dervish.

The telescope told the princes that Princess Nuronnihar ailed. They flew back to her on the magic carpet. Then they put the perfumed apple under her nose and waited to see if she would heal.

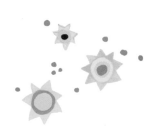

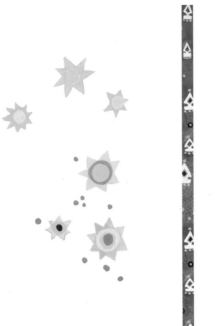

Midwives

A midwife examines a newborn baby.

In the past, in much of the world, midwives delivered babies, and in many places they still do today. In fact, midwives often tended to the full health needs of people, particularly women and children. Until recent times, midwives' knowledge was largely based on training with other midwives, and, often, on superstition and overheard information. Still, the best could be very good. Today many midwives get formal medical training, which some combine with traditional practices.

Scheherazade hushed.

"It's not yet dawn," said Shah Rayar. "You shouldn't stop yet. The story has gone all wrong. You have to fix it. Prince Hussain is right. He should have won the princess's hand. He should have won on the very first task, for the flying carpet was the most wondrous gift."

Scheherazade stayed silent; she couldn't speak in that very moment. She couldn't do anything but wait for the pain in her belly to pass.

"I have to admit I agree," said Dinarzad. "Poor Prince Hussain. He has no wife."

"But he has a flying carpet," said Scheherazade when she could speak again. "He can use it to experience other things."

"I suppose that's true," said Shah Rayar. He rubbed at the corners of his mouth. "All right. Tell me about Prince Hussain's adventures on that carpet."

"You can make them up yourself," said Scheherazade.

"What? I'm no storyteller."

Scheherazade spluttered and choked, just as Prince Hussain had done—but not from rage.

"Sister! What is it, Sister?"

"It's time."

"Time? For the baby?" Shah Rayar sat up straight. "I'll send for the midwife."

"It's coming too fast. You deliver this child."

"Me?"

Scheherazade grabbed Shah Rayar's wrist tight and gritted her teeth as her belly hardened again. When it softened, she said, "You."

"Men don't help at the births of their children."

"You are not just any man. You are king."

Shah Rayar put his free hand in his hair and pulled. "But it's wrong."

"The Almighty would want a father to take care of his child, no?"

"That's true." Now Shah Rayar put the side of his hand to his mouth and bit down on it. "But I don't know what to do. How could I possibly do this right?"

Scheherazade grabbed his other wrist tight, as another contraction came, harder than ever. When it passed,

she felt spent. *"I'll tell you what to do. Dinarzad will help."*

"This is crazy."

Scheherazade pressed the top of her head against her husband's chest as hard as she could, but it didn't lessen the pain. Still, she must not scream; she must not scare him away. "You want experience," she managed at last. "That's what you said. What could be more thrilling than helping your child enter this world?"

Shah Rayar pulled himself free. He got to his feet and stood beside the bed, staring into the dark at his wife.

Dinarzad lit a candle. She brought over the basin of water that had been waiting in the corner for this moment.

Scheherazade curled around her rock of a belly. Her moans filled the room, but her eyes remained on that husband, that husband who must must must stay.

When she fell silent again, Shah Rayar said, "Tell me what to do."

And so their second son was born, into the ready, wide, warm, and grateful hands of his father.

Shah Rayar whispered in his son's right ear the adhān—the first call to prayer. Then he held the babe to his mother's mouth and she whispered in his left ear the iqāma—the second call.

Shah Rayar wept in joy. ✳

Shah Rayar, as king, could do exceptional things. He helped his second son be born, and thus experienced one of the very best moments of his life.

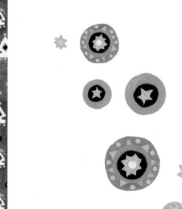

THE TALE OF ALADDIN

*"Sister, would you continue the last story now,
please," said Dinarzad. "Certainly," said Scheherazade.
"Do it quickly," said Shah Rayar. Scheherazade's heart
fluttered. She had indeed planned to finish that one quickly.
But why was her husband asking for that? What was his rush?
"Does it displease you?" "Not at all. I'm just looking forward
to the next one you'll tell tonight. The long one that will stretch
through the morning till midday." Scheherazade smiled.
"You remembered." "Two years ago tonight you told the first
story. Last year, on our first anniversary, you told an extra story:
the tale of Ali Baba and the 40 thieves. So I've been looking
forward to this second anniversary." Scheherazade laughed.
She'd been planning this anniversary tale for days. She kissed
her sons, one on her left and one on her right,
and quickly finished off the tale of the night before.
Then she plunged into the extra story.*

In far China lived the tailor Mustafa, who had a son named
Aladdin. Though the tailor and his wife were gentle people,
Aladdin was a scamp. He spent his days with loutish boys
vandalizing the property of others out of sheer boredom. After
his father died, his mother had to sell the shop, for she couldn't
run it alone. She earned a meager living by spinning cotton.

One day a magician passed through town, though no one
knew he was a magician yet. He noticed Aladdin looking
scruffy and brutish in a public square. Why, he could make use
of a boy like that. The magician asked around and learned
details about Aladdin's family. The next day he went up to
Aladdin and said, "Is your father the tailor, Mustafa?"

PREVIOUS PAGES:

*Aladdin's "uncle,"
who was really not
his uncle at all, but
a magician, led him
to a cavern under
the earth filled with
treasures of all types.
There, Aladdin found
an old, dirty lamp.*

"He died long ago."

"Oh no!" The magician burst out in tears. He clasped Aladdin to his chest. "Mustafa was my brother. You resemble him so much, it hurts to look upon you." He filled the boy's palm with coins. "Give my greetings to your mother. I will visit tomorrow, for I long to see where my beloved brother lived."

Aladdin went home confused; he'd never heard about an uncle. His mother was likewise confused.

The next day Aladdin wandered about a different section of town. Again, the magician appeared, hugged him, and gave him coins—two gold ones this time. "Take these to your mother so she can buy food. I'll come to supper tonight."

Aladdin gave the magician directions to his home and he gave the coins to his mother, who prepared an elaborate meal. The magician showed up with fruits and wines. He explained that he had been traveling for 40 years and had not seen Mustafa since they were small, but was delighted now to see his family. He asked Aladdin what trade he did.

At this, the mother berated Aladdin for his laziness.

The magician offered to set Aladdin up in a cloth shop. "Does being a merchant appeal to you, my son?"

No job appealed to Aladdin. But at least merchants dressed well. He nodded.

The next day the magician took Aladdin shopping for clothes that suited a merchant. Aladdin marched around in his new clothes. Now they needed to buy a shop and fill it with wonderful fabrics. But it would take more time to do that. So, instead, on the following day, which was a holy day, the magician took Aladdin for a walk in his new clothes so that he could meet the finest people in town and get them to agree to do business with him.

Aladdin grew excited. How lucky he was to have this marvelous uncle. They walked through fragrant gardens and talked with rich people who lived in stunning palaces. Life was like a fantasy.

They walked and walked and Aladdin gradually tired. It was hot and they had passed the edges of town. "If we keep going, I won't have the strength to walk back."

"I have something marvelous to show you. Just a little way more." The magician led Aladdin through wilderness to a valley.

"Gather brushwood for a fire, my son."

Aladdin made a fire and the magician threw incense on it. Thick smoke formed. The magician murmured a spell and the earth opened, revealing a stone slab with a bronze ring attached. The magician suddenly turned and knocked Aladdin flat on the ground with a single blow. Aladdin's mouth bled. "Why?" he cried out. "What have I done wrong?"

"Nothing. And you must do nothing wrong. I will give you directions and you must follow them exactly. The result will be wealth for us. Do you understand?" The magician's voice trembled.

Aladdin would have scoffed at such talk a few days ago. But the glitter in his uncle's eye won him over. "I will do everything you say, exactly as you say it."

"Pull on that bronze ring and lift the slab aside."

"Help me."

"Only your hands can touch it."

"I'm not strong enough to lift that by myself."

"Don't talk back! Do it!"

Aladdin grabbed the bronze ring and pulled. What! The stone came up easily, as though made of cotton. He set it aside, ever more convinced that his uncle was right about everything.

Steps descended to a door under the earth. The magician gave Aladdin instructions. He took off his ring and put it on Aladdin's finger. "This will protect you from evil."

Aladdin knew nothing of magic, so he had little faith in the ring. But he trusted his uncle, and went down the stairs, through the door. He gathered his clothes tight around him, because his uncle had warned that if any part of him touched the walls, he would die. He passed through vaulted rooms where bronze jars brimmed with gold and silver, but he took not a single pebble. Now he reached a garden where trees offered brightly colored fruits. His uncle had said he could take as many of these fruits as he liked. Aladdin touched them. Glass, he thought, though really they were diamonds, rubies, emeralds, turquoise, amethysts, and sapphires—but this humble boy knew no better. Still, he filled his shirt with them. At last he mounted a staircase and on the terrace at the top he found an old oil lamp. He blew out the flame, as his uncle had ordered, and poured

off the liquid. Then he hurried back to the cave entrance.

"Uncle," he called, laden with the glass fruits and the lamp. "Reach out a hand to help me climb up."

"Hand me the lamp first."

But something made Aladdin's old self emerge—the self who had caused his father anguish. "I'll give you the lamp once I'm out. Help me."

The more the magician insisted on having the lamp first, the more Aladdin's stubbornness grew. In a fury the magician threw incense on the fire again and uttered two magic words. Slam! The entrance to the cave shut. Aladdin was left in the dark.

The magician stomped in a circle. He was practiced in the magic of throwing pebbles in sand and learning what he wanted to know from their patterns—true geomancy. That's how he had learned of the magic lamp, which could give him all sorts of wealth. The catch was that he was not allowed to remove this lamp from the cave himself. So he had chosen Aladdin for the task. What trouble the boy had turned out to be. The magician gave up and returned to his home in a country far south.

Aladdin called out an apology to his uncle. But his voice didn't carry through the stone slab. For two days he sat on the bottom step and despaired. On the third day without food or water or sleep, he put his hands together in prayer and commended his soul to the Almighty. It was that action, simply putting his hands together, that made him inadvertently rub the ring that the magician had put on his finger and then had forgotten to take back.

A jinni appeared. "Whoever wears that ring rules me and all the other slaves of the ring. Your wish is my command."

"Get me out of here," said Aladdin. A second later he was back on the dirt outside the cave and the cave had closed, leaving no trace. He hobbled home and fell unconscious on the floor.

His mother had mourned him for dead. Now she rejoiced. When he was conscious again, she fed him tiny bit by tiny bit till he had eaten everything. Aladdin showed her the glass fruit and the lamp and told her the whole tale. Neither of them could make sense of it.

The mother went to clean the old, dirty lamp, so that Aladdin could sell it and buy more food. But with the first rub, a jinni appeared. "Whoever holds the lamp rules me and all the other slaves of the lamp. Your wish is my command." Aladdin's mother fainted.

OPPOSITE:

Hungry and thirsty, on the third day Aladdin accidentally rubbed the magician's ring in prayer. "Your wish is my command," said the monstrous jinni that appeared to him.

"Feed me," Aladdin said to the jinni.

The jinni left and returned quickly. A giant bowl and 12 plates, all of silver, all piled high with luxurious foods, were stacked on his head. In his hands were two silver cups and bottles of wine. He set all down and disappeared.

Aladdin's mother came to and looked at the food, bewildered. He told her of the jinni. She assumed it was the same jinni that had helped him escape from the cave. But, no, that was the ring jinni. This was the lamp jinni. "Get rid of that lamp!" she said. "The Almighty counsels us not to deal with jinn."

"No, Mother, I'll keep the lamp—hidden away, if you wish. I'll keep the ring as well. But to satisfy you, we'll need to find another way to get money for food."

The next day Aladdin sold one of the silver dishes to a merchant. This merchant was a scoundrel, however, and he knew a chump when he saw one. He paid Aladdin a single gold piece. Aladdin happily bought enough food for two days. Then he took another dish to the scoundrel merchant. He kept doing that till he'd sold all 12 dishes. The only thing that remained was the giant silver bowl. The merchant bought that for 10 gold pieces—a steal.

While the 10 gold pieces lasted, Aladdin spent time among the merchants, listening and becoming more worldly. When the money ran out, he called on the lamp jinni again. "Feed me," he said.

Another silver bowl. Another 12 silver dishes, two cups, food and wine. When the food was gone, Aladdin took a dish to sell to the scoundrel merchant. On the way he passed a goldsmith shop. This merchant was honest. He stopped Aladdin. "I've seen you pass with goods to sell. If you sell to me, I'll give you a just price."

Aladdin sold the dish for 72 gold pieces! He was astonished. He and his mother lived frugally for years, selling the silver dishes, one by one. In this time, Aladdin learned much by listening to the merchants. He came to recognize that the glass fruits at home were precious gems. But he didn't tell anyone.

One summer day Aladdin heard that the sultan's daughter was going to the baths and no one could look upon her as she walked the path there. Instead of shutting himself at home, like the others, Aladdin hid behind the bathhouse door. He saw the princess arrive and lift her veil.

In all his life, Aladdin had seen the face of only one woman, his mother. A plain face. But this princess was beautiful. Her eyes sparkled. Aladdin went home and suffered love pangs. He asked his mother to go to the palace and beg the sultan to let him marry the princess.

His mother laughed. Had he gone mad? Besides, even if the sultan were to grant her an audience, how could she convince him? Aladdin had done nothing to deserve the princess. And one couldn't go to the sultan without a splendid gift for him.

"Fetch your porcelain bowl, Mother." Aladdin filled it with the fruit-shaped gems he had gathered in the cave. "This is a splendid gift."

"But what will I say if he asks me about your possessions? That's all rich people care about."

"I'll find an answer. Just go, Mother. But tell no one our secrets."

Aladdin's mother went to the palace and stood in the council chamber with many others. The sultan sat on his throne and listened to everyone's problems. Aladdin's mother was intimidated. She simply watched all day, then went home. She did the same for many days, holding that porcelain bowl covered with two layers of cloth.

The sultan noticed the old woman who came so loyally but never spoke up. One evening he told his grand vizier to bring her to him the next day. When Aladdin's mother showed up in the morning, the grand vizier bid her to come forward. She bowed and touched her forehead to the carpet. When the sultan asked why she came every day, she said her son Aladdin was in love with the princess and wanted to marry her.

The sultan sighed at this silly request. But he was kind, and asked what the old woman had in her hands. She unwrapped the porcelain bowl. The sultan's mouth fell open. Glorious jewels! He said to his vizier, "This seems like the gift of a man who should marry my daughter, no?"

The grand vizier put his mouth to the sultan's ear and whispered. "You promised your daughter to my son, Your Majesty. Please put off your decision for three months and allow my son time to arrange a more valuable gift."

The sultan doubted three months would change anything. The jewels in the porcelain bowl were of immense value. But he

Modest Veils

A woman wears a veil to cover her hair, ears, mouth, and throat.

In this story, Aladdin sees the princess unveil herself and this is the first time he's seen a woman's face other than his mother's. Dressing modestly is an important Islamic principle for both men and women, and women's veils that cover the hair and sometimes the ears and throat are common today. However, women's veils that covered the whole face, with netting or a slit at the eyes to allow sight, were common in the times of this tale—not just in Muslim cultures, but in Jewish and Greek cultures, and in some areas of India, too.

didn't want to hurt his grand vizier's feelings. "Dear woman," he said to Aladdin's mother, "this is a splendid gift. It will take three months to get ready for the wedding. Tell your son to come here then."

Aladdin's mother practically glided home. She gave Aladdin the happy news. Aladdin counted the days, the hours, the minutes.

Two months later Aladdin's mother walked into town to buy oil and found the streets crowded with people in ceremonial costumes on bejeweled horses. Everyone cheered because the sultan's daughter was to marry the grand vizier's son that evening. Aladdin's mother reeled at the news. She hurried home and she and Aladdin stood there together, senseless with loss.

The magic lamp! Aladdin went to his room and rubbed it. "Jinni, tonight, when the bride and groom climb into their bed, bring the bed here, with them in it."

In a few hours the groom climbed into the wedding bed. The princess Badr al-Budur was led to the bed by her mother, the sultana, according to custom. The mother shut the door, leaving the married couple alone. The bed shook violently, rose into the air, and in an instant, they found themselves, bed and all, in the room of a strange young man, who was, of course, Aladdin.

Aladdin looked at the jinni, who was under the bed, out of sight of the princess and the groom. "Lock the groom in the privy till morning. Then bring him back."

The poor groom found himself shut in the cold, damn, stinking privy.

Aladdin climbed into bed with the princess. "Never fear. I honor and respect you. Let us sleep." He put his sword between himself and the princess, to show he had no intention of bothering her. Then he slept.

The poor princess found herself in bed in a strange room with a man beside her who clearly was berserk. She curled into the smallest ball possible. Every noise made her flinch.

In the morning Aladdin told the jinni to put the vizier's son back in the bed and carry the bed to the palace. The bed shook, rose, then plopped down in its original spot. The princess and groom didn't dare look at each other.

The groom ran to get clean and put on warm clothes to dispel the chill that had entered his bones. He had no idea what had happened, but no one should find out about it. Tense as a rabbit, he went about

Aladdin's lamp jinni carried the princess and her groom in their wedding bed to Aladdin's home. Then Aladdin banished the groom to the privy while he climbed in bed with the princess.

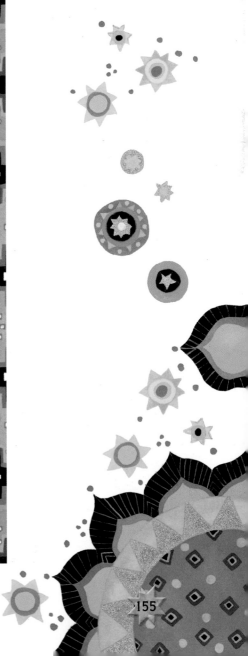

his day with a smile, pretending the night before had gone as a wedding night should.

The princess, however, huddled in bed and looked out with haunted eyes. The sultan came to her, but she refused to talk. The sultana came to her, and the princess refused again. The sultana insisted. Princess Badr al-Budur broke into tears and told the story. Horrified, her mother said, "It's good you didn't tell your father. He would think you'd lost your senses. It was only a dream." She went to the window and threw open the shutters. "Hear the trumpets, drums, tambourines? Hear the oboes, fifes, cymbals? That music is to celebrate your happiness. Put on a happy face. Act right."

That night the groom and the princess climbed into bed again, both trying to allay their fears. The same thing happened as the night before. The next morning, the groom ran off like a chicken without his head. The princess chewed on her nails and stared at her own nose.

The sultan stomped at the foot of her bed. "If you don't tell me what happened, I'll chop your head off." He unsheathed his sword.

In a gushing stream of words, the princess told everything. The sultan asked the grand vizier to see if his son would confirm the princess's tale. The grand vizier's son not only confirmed it, he begged to have the marriage annulled.

All joy in the palace ceased. All joy in the town ceased.

The sultan was flummoxed. What had caused this horror? He never once imagined that his own broken promise to Aladdin was the cause. Rather, he had totally forgotten about Aladdin. This may be hard to understand; after all, Aladdin's mother had given him the porcelain bowl filled with fantastic jewels. But the grand vizier was adept at persuasion, and he had managed to wash the sultan's mind clean of Aladdin and his old mother.

A month later, Aladdin sent his mother to the palace again, to say she had returned at the designated time—three months—and that her son was ready for marriage to the sultan's daughter. Upon seeing her, the sultan remembered his promise. But the woman was dressed so shabby that he couldn't bring himself to do the right thing. Surely, his daughter shouldn't marry a pauper. So the sultan said, "I will make good on my promise as soon as your son brings me 40 large gold bowls of jewels each on the head of a servant, with the same number

of servants leading the whole procession." An outrageous demand, to say the least.

But Aladdin rubbed his magic lamp. The next day the sultan was richer by 80 servants and by 40 bowls of pearls, emeralds, rubies, diamonds, in a procession that had made the people in the streets gawk. The bowls sat on the carpet in front of his throne. The servants stood behind them in garments fit for kings. Aladdin's mother bowed before the sultan.

The greedy sultan sent Aladdin's mother home to fetch him for a wedding that same day. He didn't ask what sort of person Aladdin was—kind or mean, intelligent or bumbling, generous or stingy, pious or impious. The sultan proved himself in that moment to be an empty-head, influenced only by wealth.

Aladdin rubbed the magic lamp and had the jinni prepare him a perfumed bath, and then the best clothes, the finest horse and saddle, harness, bridle. He ordered 40 manservants wearing silk garments. He ordered six maidservants dressed in silk and carrying six wonder-ful garments in their hands. And he ordered 10 purses, each holding a thousand pieces of gold.

Aladdin gave his mother the six maidservants and the garments they held, plus four of the bulging purses.

Then he went to the palace, with 40 servants surrounding his horse in a grand procession. Six of them scattered the gold pieces from the six remaining purses to the crowd that gathered. Though Aladdin had never been on a horse before, he rode with dignity. No one recognized the fine gentleman on horseback as the same ruffian who used to cause mischief in the public squares. And this was good, this was right, because one of the powers of the magic lamp was to make its owner as good as he deserved to be given how he used the lamp. Because Aladdin was distributing money to the townspeople, the lamp refined his soul. He was now as good a person as the best in the land.

At the palace, Aladdin prepared to kiss the ground in front of the sultan, but the sultan hugged him before he could do that. It was an aston-ishing act of friendship. Remember, this sultan was a fool for displays of wealth; nothing could have made him happier than seeing all these well-dressed servants around this man who seemed to exhale money.

Aladdin and the sultan ate together, and Aladdin asked to put off the

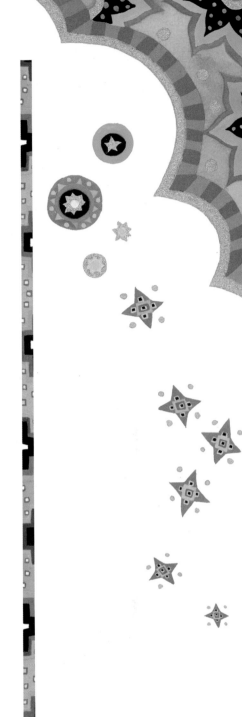

OPPOSITE:

Aladdin had his lamp jinni build an astonishingly lavish palace, with many levels and all sorts of the finest jewels and stones. It was so near the sultan's palace, the sultan could look upon it easily.

wedding long enough to build a palace to live in. The sultan agreed and gave Aladdin a large plot of land close to his own palace.

Aladdin returned home and, of course, rubbed the magic lamp. The jinni summoned all the other jinn within the lamp—all slaves of the lamp. By morning a new palace stood beside the sultan's, made of all the best materials: porphyry, lapis lazuli, jasper, agate, and marble in every color. On the top was a square room, with six windows on each side, and a dome on top. Jewel-laden lattices covered the windows, all but one, that was left unfinished. The new palace had a garden behind, a courtyard within, and a forecourt. It had a kitchen, pantries, storehouses, halls, bedrooms, a treasure room filled with gold. It had stables with fast steeds and skilled riders, trained grooms, much hunting equipment. Last of all, Aladdin had a fine velvet carpet stretched out from the front gate of the sultan's palace to the front gate of the new palace.

When the sultan woke and saw this palace, he grew giddy with delight. The grand vizier said, "A palace built in a single night? Magic is afoot!" But the sultan chalked the grand vizier's reaction up to envy.

That night there was a sumptuous feast, with music and dance. Then Princess Badr al-Budur kissed her parents goodbye and walked the velvet carpet to the new palace, where Aladdin awaited her. He had made his jinni prepare a special meal, in dishes and goblets of exquisite craftsmanship. The bride and groom ate with Aladdin's mother, while musicians played, women sang, and dancers twirled around them. Finally, Aladdin took his bride to their wedding bed.

Aladdin was kind and sweet to the princess that night. He won her love, for nothing is as irresistible as being adored.

The next morning Aladdin invited the sultan to dine in the new palace. The sultan walked through the halls, exclaiming at their beauty. But he asked why one window on the top floor was left unfinished. Aladdin smiled. "This way you can have the pleasure of finishing it, and thus finishing the whole palace. I can be suitably grateful every time I look at the palace, since without your consent, none of this would have happened."

The sultan loved the idea. He called together the best jewelers to make the final window lattice immediately. Little did he realize that the kind of workmanship that had gone into the other window lattices was beyond what any human could do. His men worked for a month, and

used up nearly all the jewels in the sultan's treasury, yet still they hadn't finished even half the job.

Aladdin realized that his idea wasn't turning out right. So he made the sultan's workers undo everything and return the jewels to the treasury. Then he rubbed the magic lamp and had the jinn of the lamp make a lattice for the window.

When the workers told the sultan that Aladdin had sent them away, the sultan came running to find out why. He could hardly believe his eyes; the lattice was now finished. "You're a marvel, Aladdin."

But the grand vizier said nothing, convinced this was evil magic.

Several years went by. In this time, Aladdin got to know everyone in town, and gave gold pieces to those in need. He became so beloved that people adopted the custom of invoking his name when they made promises.

While all this was going on, the magician who had tricked Aladdin in the first place was living in his home when one day, for no particular reason, he wondered about that stubborn boy Aladdin, who he had left in the cave. He took out the square box he used for geomancy and smoothed the sand in it. Then he threw a handful of beads into the air and studied the pattern they made when they fell onto the sand. What was this! Aladdin wasn't dead. To the contrary, he was a rich man, married to a princess.

Surely it was the work of the magic lamp. The stupid boy had discovered its powers. The magician rode horseback day and night, moon after moon. He arrived in Aladdin's town in China and took a room at the best public inn. He walked around and discovered the new palace, which was of such splendor it could only have been constructed by jinn. He learned from passersby that Aladdin was on a hunting trip. Excellent. Aladdin's absence was the magician's opportunity.

He went to a store and had 12 oil lamps made, polished to a shine. The next day he walked through town, crying, "Lamps, lamps, lamps to trade. Give me your old, I'll give you my new." People laughed; such a trade made no sense.

One of the princess's maidservants heard him and thought of the old lamp that Aladdin kept on a shelf. Wouldn't it be a nice surprise for Aladdin if they made this trade? The princess agreed. She sent a manservant to make the trade.

The magician had never seen the magic lamp before, of course. But he had no doubt that the old lamp this palace servant held was the magic lamp. He made the trade and ran out of town, through the wilderness, to a secluded spot. Then he rubbed it.

The jinni appeared. "Whoever holds the lamp rules me and all the other slaves of the lamp. Your wish is my command."

"Transport me and the entire palace with everyone within it, to my home country."

Instantly, all was exactly as the magician had ordered.

Back in China, the sultan walked by his window, casually glancing out. He rubbed his eyes. He shouted. The grand vizier came running. "Do you see the palace of my daughter and Aladdin?"

The grand vizier rubbed his own eyes. "It's disappeared." He slapped his fist into his palm. "I knew there was magic afoot!"

"Bring Aladdin to me, and I'll have his head chopped off!"

So horsemen rode out to the countryside and surrounded Aladdin. They put a chain around him and led him back to the palace. When the townspeople saw him bound like this, they grew angry. This was their hero. They demanded he be set free.

The sultan saw that the splendid palace where his daughter lived had disappeared. His vizier's suspicions were confirmed: Aladdin had conspired with magic forces.

The guards stopped the townsfolk at the palace gate and brought Aladdin into the forecourt. From outside the crowds shouted. They gathered arms to storm the palace.

"If you kill Aladdin," said the grand vizier, "you risk everything, Your Majesty. The people love him."

The sultan shook in terror, for the mob grew larger. He turned to his guards. "Tell the people I pardon Aladdin."

So the guards unbound Aladdin and the crowds dispersed.

Aladdin stood outside the palace and called up to the sultan. "Won't you tell me the crime I am accused of?"

"Come up here and I'll show you," called back the sultan. When Aladdin had entered and climbed the stairs to the balcony, the sultan jabbed his finger in the air. "See?"

Aladdin blinked. "Where is my palace?"

"More important, where is my daughter?"

Aladdin put his hands in his hair and rocked back and forth on his feet. How could he have lost the woman he loved? "Give me 40 days to find my dearest princess. If I don't succeed, kill me, for I won't want to live." And he raced away.

He asked everyone if they knew what had become of the princess. None could help. He wandered through the countryside. Despair weighed him down. He didn't eat or sleep. He stopped by the river and stared at it. The only solution was to take his own life by drowning.

First, though, he would pray. He went down the steep slope that led to the river, where he would wash before prayer, but his foot slipped and he tumbled against a rock. In the process he accidentally rubbed his ring. The ring jinni appeared.

Aladdin had forgotten about the powers of the ring, for the magic lamp had taken care of his needs for years. "Oh, wonderful jinni. Bring back my palace and my wife."

"I am but the slave of the ring. You must speak with the slave of the lamp for that request."

"Then take me to my palace. Set me down under the window of my precious wife."

A moment later Aladdin found himself outside the palace he knew so well. It was darkest night. He collapsed in a heap of fatigue. At dawn he woke and looked up at the princess's window. His mind was clear for the first time since he'd been arrested by the sultan. He realized now that the palace had been brought here by the magic of his old lamp. Someone had found it. His insides went cold with dread. Who else could it be but that magician who pretended to be his uncle?

When the princess appeared at her window, Aladdin called up to her. In joy, she had a servant open the secret door below her room. Aladdin came up and their tears mingled. Aladdin explained what he thought must have happened. Princess Badr al-Budur told him about the trade of the lamp, and how the magician carried that old lamp with him constantly. He visited her every day and wanted her to marry him, but she would have nothing to do with him.

A plan formed in Aladdin's head. He went out the secret door and found a peasant to exchange clothes with. Then he went to the street with all the apothecary shops and bought a special powder. He returned to the princess. "Trust me. I need you to do something that will be abhorrent to you. But it will turn good in the end."

The princess did as Aladdin asked. She bathed and perfumed herself. She had a maidservant arrange her hair beautifully. She put on her fanciest dress. She draped herself with jewelry. When the magician came, she smiled at him sweetly.

He stumbled a few steps backward. "Your change in attitude … ah, princess … it surprises me."

"I am a practical person," said the princess. "I have faced the fact that Aladdin is dead by now. My father will have slain him. Today I performed the final rites for him, everything a widow should do. Now I must look to the future." She nodded at him solemnly. "With you." He nodded back, his face all delight. "I have ordered a special supper," said the princess. "We should drink wine, too. All I have is wine from my old home. I wish I had the best local wine to offer."

"There are wonderful local wines in my storeroom," said the magician. "I'll get them." He raced off, just as the princess had hoped.

She took out two goblets and in one she put the powder that Aladdin had bought at the apothecary. When the magician returned, the princess brought over the two goblets she had set aside and handed the magician the empty one, keeping the one with the powder for herself. She poured wine in both of them and went to put hers to her lips. She stopped midway, as though thoughtful. "In China when people are lovers, they

exchange goblets. Why don't you drink from mine and I, from yours?"

The magician slapped a palm over his heart. "I never dreamed we could find such happiness."

They drank, and the magician fell dead from the poison powder.

Aladdin came up the stairs and found the magic lamp inside the magician's shirt. He rubbed it and ordered the jinni to transport the palace back to China. An instant later they were there. Only moments after that the sultan came running in, astonished and relieved. Aladdin had the magician's corpse thrown in a dunghill for wild animals to rip apart. The whole town celebrated the return of Aladdin and Princess Badr al-Budur in a 10-day-long festival. So the magic ring on Aladdin's finger had saved him a second time.

Soon after that, the magician's younger brother, who had been traveling, returned home for their annual reunion. When the magician didn't show up, his brother suspected trouble. He also was skilled in geomancy. He took out his box, leveled the sand, and made his throw. The figures in the sand were clear: the magician had died, poisoned by a man who now lived in China married to a sultan's daughter. He set out immediately for vengeance, across deserts, rivers, plains, mountains. When he arrived in Aladdin's town, he walked about trying to figure out a plan for killing him.

He learned of a woman named Fatima who was so pious, she could heal others. They said she went out only on certain days, but if he waited, he'd be sure to see her. He didn't wait. He went to her home that night and put a dagger to her throat. "Wake up, old woman. Don't scream." Fatima's eyes flew open. "You must do me a favor and I will not harm you. Exchange clothes with me. Then paint my face so I look like you." Fatima did as the magician's brother ordered. She even put on him the long string of beads she always wore. The magician strangled her and threw her body down a cistern.

In the morning, he went out dressed as Fatima, with a veil over his head. People were surprised to see Fatima out on a day when she usually stayed at home. They clamored after her, begging her to make this one's wound close up, that one's fever cool down, another one's cough disappear.

The princess was in her room at the top of the house. She heard the street noise and asked her servants to bring up the holy lady.

Healing Power

A medieval healer formulates and mixes potions and ointments.

The woman Fatima in this tale is known as very pious, and it is this characteristic that makes her a healer. From ancient times up through medieval times—and in some places into modern times—we find the belief that healers' abilities come from devotion to the divine or even collaboration with the divine. This belief is not limited to any one society or type of society, but appears throughout the world.

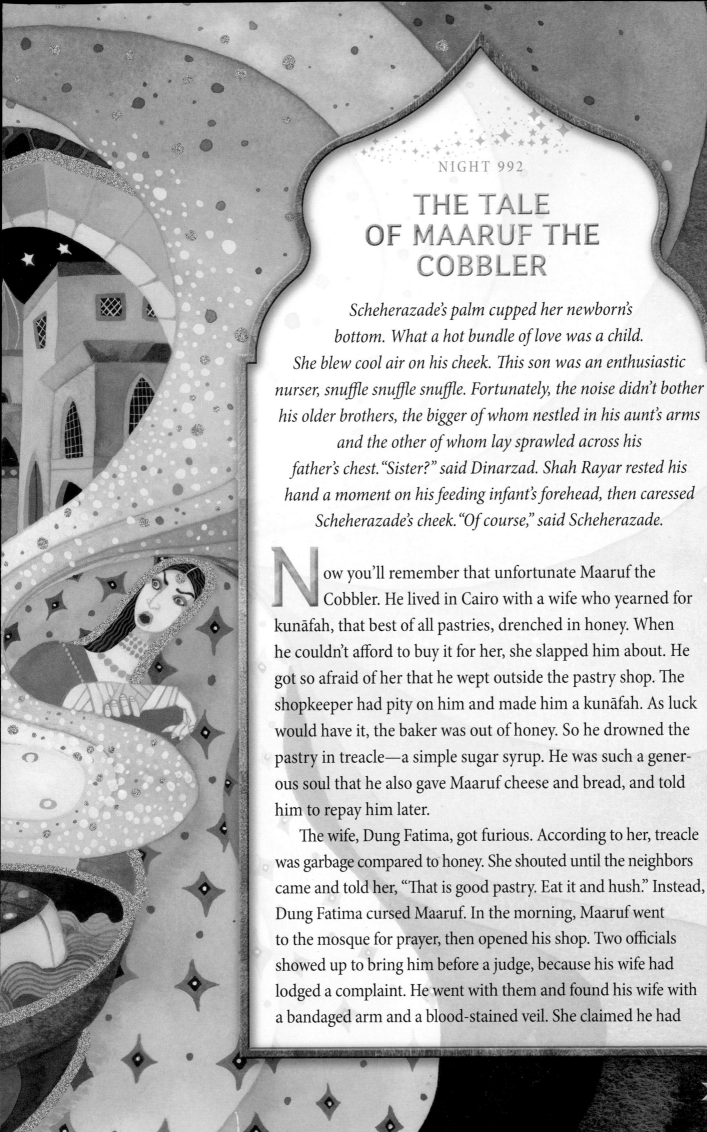

THE TALE OF MAARUF THE COBBLER

*Scheherazade's palm cupped her newborn's
bottom. What a hot bundle of love was a child.
She blew cool air on his cheek. This son was an enthusiastic
nurser, snuffle snuffle snuffle. Fortunately, the noise didn't bother
his older brothers, the bigger of whom nestled in his aunt's arms
and the other of whom lay sprawled across his
father's chest. "Sister?" said Dinarzad. Shah Rayar rested his
hand a moment on his feeding infant's forehead, then caressed
Scheherazade's cheek. "Of course," said Scheherazade.*

Now you'll remember that unfortunate Maaruf the Cobbler. He lived in Cairo with a wife who yearned for kunāfah, that best of all pastries, drenched in honey. When he couldn't afford to buy it for her, she slapped him about. He got so afraid of her that he wept outside the pastry shop. The shopkeeper had pity on him and made him a kunāfah. As luck would have it, the baker was out of honey. So he drowned the pastry in treacle—a simple sugar syrup. He was such a generous soul that he also gave Maaruf cheese and bread, and told him to repay him later.

The wife, Dung Fatima, got furious. According to her, treacle was garbage compared to honey. She shouted until the neighbors came and told her, "That is good pastry. Eat it and hush." Instead, Dung Fatima cursed Maaruf. In the morning, Maaruf went to the mosque for prayer, then opened his shop. Two officials showed up to bring him before a judge, because his wife had lodged a complaint. He went with them and found his wife with a bandaged arm and a blood-stained veil. She claimed he had

PREVIOUS PAGES:

Maaruf's wife was so awful to him that a jinni who lived in a ruined wall had pity on him and granted him a wish. Naturally, Maaruf's wish was to escape from his wife.

Arab Cuisine

Kunāfah is a sweet dessert made of thin pastry and honey.

The traditional pastry in this story dates back to Syria and Muslim Spain in the 13th century. Over the next 400 to 500 years the Ottoman Empire spread from Turkey northwest into Europe along the Mediterranean Sea as far as Slovenia, and southwest across the lands of northern Africa bordering the Mediterranean Sea all the way into Morocco. It also spread east to the Caspian Sea. This empire accounts for certain similarities in cuisine among disparate cultures, although local variations on common dishes abound.

broken her arm and knocked out her tooth.

Stunned, Maaruf explained what had really happened. The judge, who was a good man and wanted to reconcile them, gave Maaruf money to buy kunāfah made with honey. The officers then demanded Maaruf pay for their services. Alas, he had to sell his tools to pay them, and, of course, he couldn't work without his tools. The next thing he knew, his wife had lodged another complaint against him. And on it went, getting worse, until the wife lodged a complaint in the High Court. This was serious! The bailiff was coming for him. Maaruf fled, not even paying attention to where he was going.

A storm came up and soaked the cobbler. He went into a deserted building, leaned against a ruined wall, and wept. All at once a tall, grotesque, ghostlike figure stood before him. "I am the jinni of the wall. You seem a pathetic thing, so I will grant you a wish." Maaruf asked to be taken far away, where his wife's complaints could do him no harm.

Just like that, he found himself on a mountaintop. He went down into the city below. People laughed at his strange clothes and asked where he came from. Maaruf said, "I left Cairo only a little while ago." They scoffed and called him a liar, for Cairo was a year's journey away.

A merchant came up and told the small crowd that had gathered to stop making fun of the stranger and disperse. Then he took Maaruf home, gave him clothes, and fed him. The merchant asked where he had really come from. When Maaruf said Cairo again, it turned out that this merchant was also from Cairo. He asked if Maaruf knew a certain apothecary. Well he did, for this was Maaruf's neighbor. The merchant asked what had become of the apothecary's children. Maaruf gave an account of two of the sons, but one, a certain Ali who had been his childhood friend, had run away after his father had punished him for a boyish prank they had pulled together. The merchant hugged Maaruf, for he was none other than the long-lost Ali.

Scheherazade went silent. She had thought she'd never be grateful for the dawn again, but her energy was low these days. Being the mother of three boys—a toddler, a crawler, and a newborn—was

*taking its toll. Falling silent felt very good. Dinarzad didn't say a word.
"Ali being there is a remarkable coincidence," said Shah Rayar.
"That's what a man needs when his wife is awful—
happy coincidence." He reached an arm around his wife and
cuddled her close as they fell back asleep.* ✳

THE TALE OF MAARUF
THE COBBLER CONTINUES

*No one was sleeping well tonight. The heat made them restless.
So why wait for Dinarzad's call? Scheherazade arranged her sons on
her stomach like puppies in a pile and began.*

Maaruf the Cobbler from Cairo was now in a new land,
grateful to have met his childhood friend Ali by chance.
He told what had happened to bring him here.

Ali then told Maaruf his own tale. When he came here, to Ikhtiyan
al-Khutan, he was hardly more than a boy with nothing in his purse.
He told people he was a merchant, whose goods were following. He
asked them to clear a place where he could store them and to lend
him money until they arrived. The people were of a generous, trust-
ing mind-set, and they did that. Ali bought goods with the money and
sold them at the market. Before long he had earned enough to pay
back his debtors and still had some left to become a real merchant.
Now he was a well-respected merchant with many friends. "Swagger
is the trick. If you tell people the truth about yourself—that you ran
away from a mean wife—you'll be a laughingstock. But since they
don't know you, you can tell them whatever you like. With a confident
air. I'll back you up on anything you say."

This seemed sensible to Maaruf.

The next day Ali gave Maaruf a thousand dinars, a mule to ride,
and a servant to precede him. Then Maaruf rode the mule slowly
to the merchants' market. Ali had already arrived there. As Maaruf
approached, Ali jumped up from his circle of friends and said, "Blessed
day! Here is my friend Maaruf, the fabulously successful merchant."

He went on and on about how generous and rich Maaruf was.

Then he asked Maaruf if he had yellow broadcloth, a fabric much prized in the city. Maaruf answered as they had rehearsed: "I have lengths and lengths of it." And did he have cloth the red color of gazelle blood? "Lengths and lengths" said Maaruf. He had thousands of fabrics, all following with his servants.

As they sat there, a beggar came by. Maaruf gave him a handful of gold. Another came, and yet another. Each went away with a handful of gold, until the entire thousand dinars was gone. Then Maaruf lamented that he'd brought only that small amount of money with him. What would he do now if another beggar came along? He couldn't bear to turn anyone away empty-handed. One of Ali's friends lent Maaruf another thousand dinars. Maaruf gave this money away, too. Beggars and merchants alike were astonished at his generosity. One after another, the merchants lent Maaruf a thousand dinars, and he gave it all away. By the time of afternoon prayer, Maaruf had borrowed 5,000 dinars and given it all away.

The next day was a repeat. And the next. By the end of 20 days, Maaruf had borrowed 60,000 dinars, and given every coin to beggars. His goods—which, of course, didn't exist—hadn't appeared yet. Ali warned Maaruf that he was playing his role too well. How on earth could he pay back such a huge sum and why did he have to keep giving it all away?

But Maaruf told him, "Don't worry. When my goods arrive, I'll pay back everyone double what they gave me."

"Are you crazy?" said Ali. "You have no goods."

"Of course I do," said Maaruf.

By now Ali was worried that the merchants who had lent Maaruf money would be angry at him for introducing Maaruf to them. So he told the merchants they mustn't blame him if things went wrong because he had never advised them to lend Maaruf money.

Morning came, thank heavens. Scheherazade stopped, exhausted again. "Swagger might be a good trick," said Shah Rayar, "but I agree with Ali. This Maaruf has gone too far. He's made a mess of things." "Really?" said Scheherazade. "What has he done but take money from rich merchants and distribute it to the poor?" Shah Rayar pursed his lips. ✳

173

THE TALE OF MAARUF THE COBBLER CONTINUES

*Had Maaruf gone too far? And had Scheherazade,
therefore, gone too far? Her sister stayed silent—
that wasn't a good sign. The girl must agree with
Scheherazade's husband. Ah, well, what could she do? She was
mired in the story now. She had to trust that somehow she'd
manage to turn events in a way that pleased the king.
So the next night she picked up where she'd left off.*

When Maaruf's goods didn't come, the merchants he
owed money to feared he was a cheat. They asked
the king to rescue them. The king listened to the description of
Maaruf's behavior. This didn't seem like a bad man; he seemed
like a man of immeasurable wealth. His vizier didn't agree;
Maaruf was a fraudster for sure.

The king decided to test Maaruf. He summoned him to the
palace and put a gem in his hand. He told Maaruf to identify
it and say its worth. A rich man could do that, a poor couldn't.
Maaruf squeezed the gem and it shattered. "This was no gem,"
said Maaruf, "but a mineral, worth only a thousand dinars."
The king blinked. How could anyone think a thousand dinars
was a small sum?

"A real jewel," said Maaruf, "is worth 70,000. When my
baggage comes, I will give you real jewels as gifts."

The delighted king was convinced. Soon he told his vizier
to offer the princess's hand in marriage to this Maaruf. The
vizier objected still. But the king accused him of envy, because
the vizier had offered to marry the princess himself and she
had refused him. So the vizier had no choice but to ask Maaruf

PREVIOUS PAGES:

*The king suspected
Maaruf was a
trickster. So he tested
him by asking him to
judge the value of a
gem. Maaruf crushed
the gem and called
it worthless.*

if he would marry the princess. Maaruf agreed; as soon as his goods arrived they would marry. Then he could shower the princess with riches, as befit her, and he could give money to the poor, as befit the husband of the princess.

The king would have no delay, though. After all, his treasury was full. Maaruf could use the king's money until his goods arrived.

The wedding celebrations went on for 40 days. Maaruf scattered gold on everyone he saw, winning the love of the populace. He gave robes of honor to the officers of state and distributed gifts, winning the love of the rich. Most important, he won the love of the princess. Everything was going perfectly.

Time passed and Maaruf's goods never appeared. Meanwhile, Maaruf gave money away lavishly until the king's treasury was nearly depleted. The vizier told the king Maaruf would bring ruin upon them all. So the king called his daughter in for questioning. After all, if anyone knew the truth about Maaruf, it would be her. The princess knew only that Maaruf made promises of wealth to come. So the king asked her to get him to talk with her frankly. The princess agreed.

That night the princess called Maaruf the heat of love's passion. She hugged him tight. And she begged him to tell her the truth of his situation.

He did. Every detail. He confessed he had no idea how to extricate himself from all his lies.

The princess told him that her father suspected him and would certainly have him put to death. Yet she loved Maaruf as she had never guessed a woman could love a man. She gave him a horse and 50,000 dinars of her own money to escape. He promised the princess that he would send a message once he was living someplace safe. She promised that when her father died, she would send for him and he could be king.

*Scheherazade held up her hand to the stream of light from the
window. Already she could see the sun would scorch that day.
"Stay inside with us today, Husband."
"Business calls me," he said quietly, his voice raspy.
"You sound sad."
"Maaruf, scoundrel that he is, holds the adoration of the princess.
To her he is the heat of love's passion." Shah Rayar lowered his chin so*

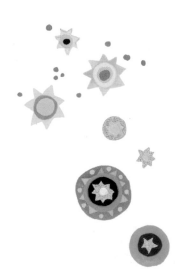

that his eyes looked up searchingly into his wife's. "What am I to you?"
"The beat of my heart."
Shah Rayar smiled. "Good." ✳

THE TALE OF MAARUF
THE COBBLER CONTINUES

"I'm glad Maaruf wasn't really crazy," said Dinarzad. "I worried
he really thought his goods were coming. After all, borrowing
so much and giving it all away with no thought to his day of
reckoning made him seem addled."
"I agree," said the king.
"But riding away won't solve things," said
Dinarzad. "What about the merchants he borrowed from?"
"And the king's depleted treasury?" said Shah Rayar.
"What impatient people I live with," said Scheherazade. "Listen."

Maaruf the Cobbler rode away on the princess's horse dressed
as a king's servant. In the morning, the princess went to her
father with a letter she said had been delivered to her by Maaruf's
servants, but which, of course, she had written herself, for she was
educated. The letter declared that it came from the 500 servants
in Maaruf's retinue. They had been attacked by Bedouin, who stole
200 loads of fabrics and killed 50 of them.

The princess said Maaruf was baffled: How could his servants have
been so foolish as to fight over a mere 200 loads of fabric? They should
have given the goods to the Bedouin. Oh, this princess was as fine
a liar as Maaruf himself! She said she watched from the window as
Maaruf rushed off to his remaining men and she saw those messenger
servants. Their robes glowed like moonlight, more splendidly than
anything the king had.

The king believed his daughter. What a mistaken wretch that vizier
was. Yes, yes, all should be patient until Maaruf returned.

Meanwhile, Maaruf rode fast, tears forming a streak behind him,
for he was miserable. Yes, he wanted to live, but how bitter it was to leave
this dear wife, his sweet delight. He rode through the night and didn't

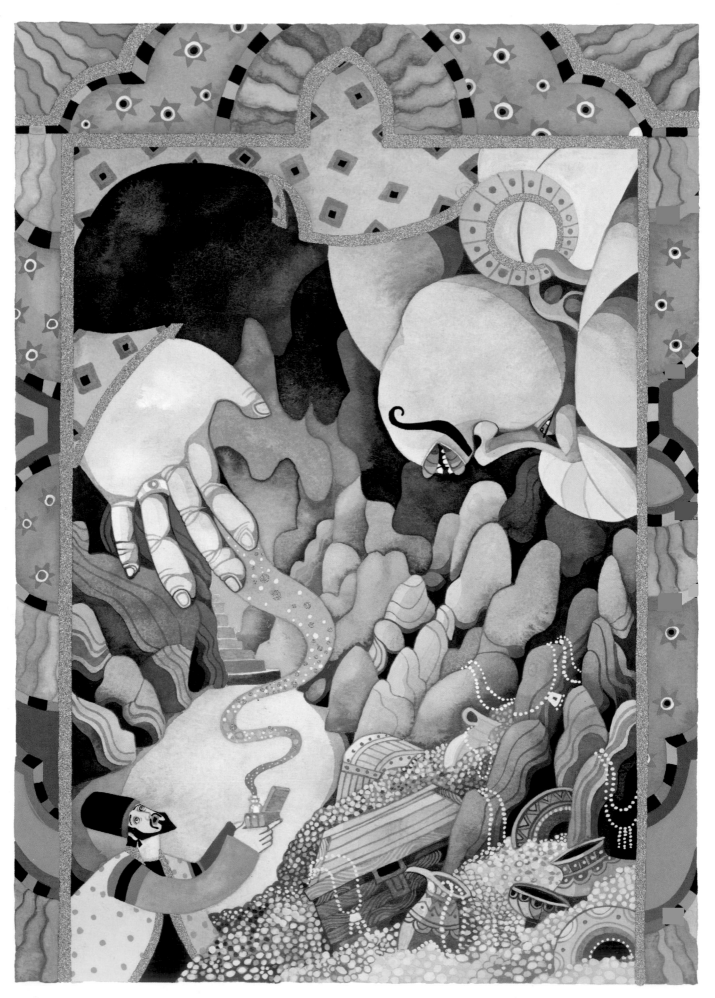

stop till noon, when he saw a peasant plowing with two oxen. The peasant took one look at Maaruf's grief-stricken face and told him to rest while he ran to the village for food. Then they would share a restoring meal.

Maaruf sat a moment to rest, when he realized the peasant was giving up his work in order to help a stranger. So he took up the plow and continued working the field. After only moments, the oxen stopped and wouldn't budge. Maaruf checked the plow. Why, it was caught on a gold ring. He cleared away dirt and saw the ring was set in a marble slab. He shoved until that slab moved enough for him to see steps behind it, going down. He descended into an enormous underground hall with four side chambers: one filled with gold; one with emeralds, corals, and pearls; one with turquoises, sapphires, and hyacinth jewels; one with diamonds. In the main hall was a crystal chest full of gems he didn't recognize, and on top was a gold box that fit in his palm. He opened it. A gold ring sat there, inscribed with a graceful script. He rubbed it to see better.

"Master, what is your wish?" came a voice.

"Who are you?" asked Maaruf.

"I'm the servant of the ring. I will do whatever you ask, no matter how difficult, for I am lord of the jinn and I command thousands upon thousands of jinn."

Sun warmed Scheherazade. She put
a finger in a curl of her middle son's hair.
"I thought this cobbler a fool," said Shah Rayar haltingly. "Yet
now fate seems about to reward him. Perhaps he has some substance
to him. After all, he understood something as though he was wise."
"And what was that, dear husband?"
"He knew his wife was his sweet delight."
Scheherazade's breath caught.
"You are my sweet delight," said Shah Rayar.
Could it be? The dawn before, when Scheherazade said Shah Rayar
was the beat of her heart, she meant it literally, for he determined if
she lived or died. But maybe she meant it in other ways, too. For his words
now melted her. She pressed her nose to his cheek and breathed in the
musty, nutty, woody scent that emanated from this man, and
she realized that scent cradled her soul. ✳

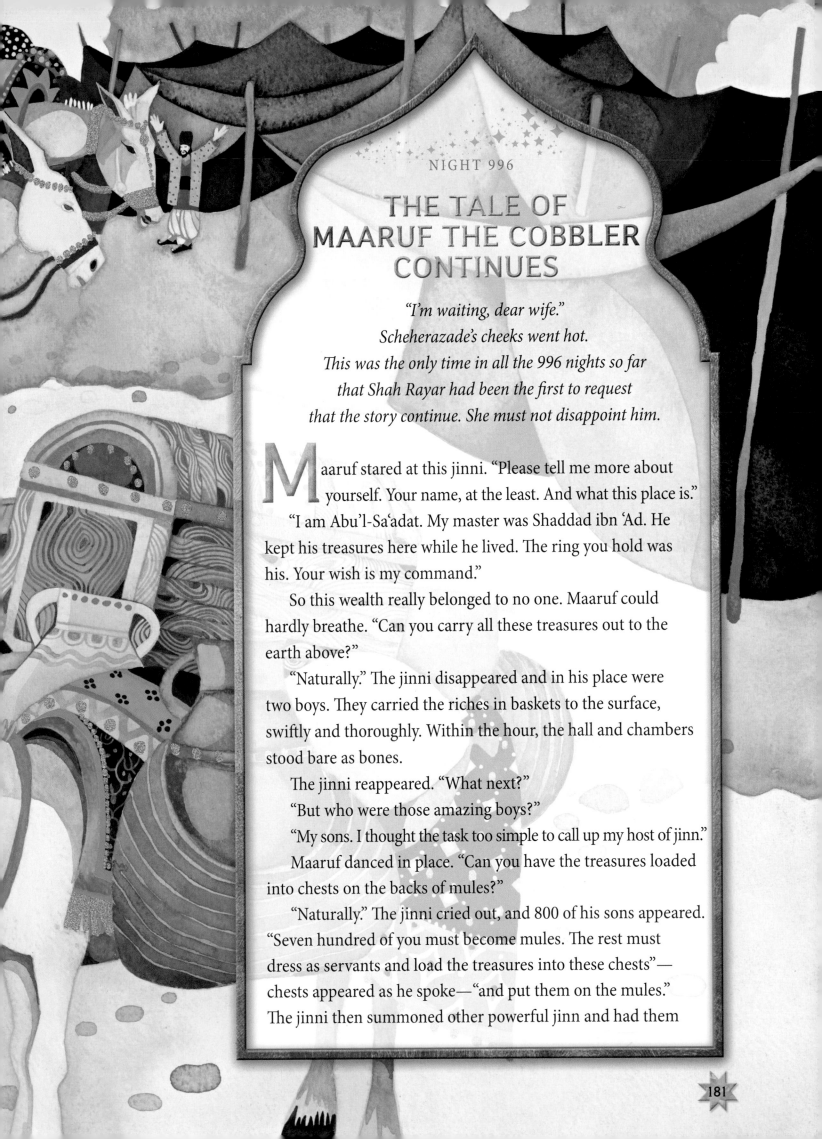

THE TALE OF MAARUF THE COBBLER CONTINUES

"I'm waiting, dear wife."
Scheherazade's cheeks went hot.
This was the only time in all the 996 nights so far
that Shah Rayar had been the first to request
that the story continue. She must not disappoint him.

Maaruf stared at this jinni. "Please tell me more about yourself. Your name, at the least. And what this place is."

"I am Abu'l-Sa'adat. My master was Shaddad ibn 'Ad. He kept his treasures here while he lived. The ring you hold was his. Your wish is my command."

So this wealth really belonged to no one. Maaruf could hardly breathe. "Can you carry all these treasures out to the earth above?"

"Naturally." The jinni disappeared and in his place were two boys. They carried the riches in baskets to the surface, swiftly and thoroughly. Within the hour, the hall and chambers stood bare as bones.

The jinni reappeared. "What next?"

"But who were those amazing boys?"

"My sons. I thought the task too simple to call up my host of jinn."

Maaruf danced in place. "Can you have the treasures loaded into chests on the backs of mules?"

"Naturally." The jinni cried out, and 800 of his sons appeared. "Seven hundred of you must become mules. The rest must dress as servants and load the treasures into these chests"— chests appeared as he spoke—"and put them on the mules." The jinni then summoned other powerful jinn and had them

PREVIOUS PAGES:

The jinni had 700 of his sons turn into mules. Then another 100 sons piled the treasures into chests and loaded the chests onto the backs of those mules.

Nomads vs. City Dwellers

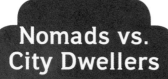

A Bedouin leads camels across the desert.

In the fourth through sixth centuries, the caravan trade was secured by the Bedouin, a nomadic people who didn't belong to any settled community. They saw city life as a threat and fought to return many areas to pastureland. This tension between the Bedouin and city people only increased as Islam spread across the Arab world, since the Bedouin did not want to give up their beliefs in multiple gods and their tribal ways and customs. Today Bedouin people maintain much of their poetry, music, dance, and food culture, but few are still nomadic.

turn into fine horses with gold bejeweled saddles.

"I need bales of fabric, too," said Maaruf.

"From Rum, India, Persia, Syria, or Egypt?" asked the jinni.

"One hundred bales from each, every bale on a mule."

"All will be ready by dawn," said the jinni. Then he made a tent appear with a food-laden table.

The peasant who had gone off to the village to fetch food now returned with a humble bowl of lentils for the stranger and a bag of barley for his horse. He stood stunned at the sight of the tent and all the mules with treasure chests on their backs.

"Welcome back," said Maaruf. "Let me eat the lentils you have so kindly provided, while you eat the food on this table."

That's what they did. When Maaruf emptied the lentil bowl, he filled it with gold. "This is meager thanks for your hospitality. Please visit me in the palace whenever you come to the city, and I will host you."

Dancing girls appeared and entertained Maaruf until he slept. In the morning, hundreds of mules carrying hundreds of bales of cloth arrived at his tent, preceded by a palanquin held by four men. It was full of luxurious robes. This way Maaruf could arrive back at the palace with a procession more extravagant than any before.

Maaruf gave the jinni a letter and asked him to race ahead in the form of a courier and bring it to the king. Off went the jinni.

Moments later the jinni burst into the king's throne room. The king was just telling his vizier how worried he was that Maaruf might have been killed by the Bedouin and the vizier was, of course, responding that Maaruf was a complete fraudster. They jumped back in surprise at this messenger. "Your Majesty," said the jinni. "Here is a letter from your son-in-law, who will arrive soon with his baggage retinue."

"Didn't I tell you?" said the king to the vizier. "You're the scoundrel, not Maaruf." He had the town decorated for Maaruf's arrival.

*Scheherazade eased down into the pillows.
"Dawn comes too soon," said Dinarzad. "What will Maaruf's wife think now?"
"And what will become of that vizier? He's done his best.*

And, in truth, he was right. No one can predict when the Almighty will help right a situation."

"Must we wait for the coming night to learn more?" asked Dinarzad. But Scheherazade kept her eyes closed. ✷

THE TALE OF MAARUF THE COBBLER CONTINUES

Scheherazade gently bounced her middle son on her knees. He had a tummy ache, and the pressure and motion gave the little one comfort. She knew her voice would soothe him, too, so she didn't wait to be invited to speak.

The king rushed to tell his daughter the good news of her husband's return. The princess didn't know what to think. She waited, with equal amounts of joy and anxiety.

Ali, Maaruf's childhood friend, also had mixed feelings. He prayed that Maaruf should not be shamed at whatever was to happen next.

The merchants, however, were thoroughly delighted, for they would be repaid at last.

Far away, Maaruf climbed into the palanquin and headed for the palace. Halfway there, the king and his retinue met him. At the sight of all Maaruf's horses, mules, servants, and goods, rapture filled the king, for riches impressed him to no end. Together they formed a giant procession back to town.

The merchants cheered. Ali caught Maaruf's ear for a moment and congratulated him on pulling off this enormous hoax, for his generosity showed he deserved to succeed.

Maaruf entered the palace and immediately he had his goods brought to him, bale by bale, chest by chest. He gave treasures away to all the palace servants. He repaid the merchants twice what they had lent him. He gave money to the poor and precious stones to the soldiers. He filled the royal treasury to overflowing.

The king said, "Be careful to save some for yourself, Maaruf."

But Maaruf paid no heed. After all, the jinni Abu'l-Sa'adat could always fetch him more of anything he might ever want.

Not a soul in the kingdom remained unastonished at his generosity.

Finally, Maaruf went to see his wife in her private chamber. She kissed him and laughed, but her eyes were steady. "You are wealthy, my husband, beyond anyone's imagination. Yet you told me it was all a hoax. You said you were penniless and without any idea of what to do next. Were you toying with me? Or were you testing my love?" Her eyes brimmed with tears, for either answer would hurt her.

"Never would I toy with you." Maaruf closed her hands in his. He had done neither of the things she asked, but right now was not the moment to explain that. "You proved yourself sincere. You love me genuinely, regardless of worldly goods. Integrity shines through you. No one ever has been or ever will be as dear to me as you are."

The next chance Maaruf had to be alone, he rubbed the ring and the jinni appeared. He asked for robes for his beloved wife with jewelry to adorn her from hair to toes and a necklace set with 40 gems. The jinni brought them and thus Maaruf carried them to his wife. Oh, how the princess loved them, especially the golden anklets. But she declared them too fine for daily use; she'd save them for festivals. Of course, Maaruf wouldn't hear of that. He said he'd get her even better wear for festivals. When the princess's maidservants saw the princess decked out, they gasped. So Maaruf had the jinni bring robes and jewelry for all of them, as well.

When the vizier saw servants dressed better than most royalty anywhere in the world, he went to the king. "You must listen. This kind of wealth has roots in magic. How can it be otherwise? Please please listen to me. We must invite Maaruf to drink wine with us, and when we have him thoroughly inebriated, we can get him to tell us the truth."

The king's mouth twisted in doubt.

"Please, Your Majesty," said the vizier. Right now everyone loves him. If he decides he wants to overthrow you, I fear even the army would do his bidding. You can't afford to ignore me."

The first day's drop of sweat glistened on Shah Rayar's eager face. Scheherazade went silent.
"So the vizier will win, after all," said the king.
Scheherazade laughed. "Guess all you want, but for the story you'll have to wait till the coming night." ✳

OPPOSITE: *Maaruf had the jinni bring beautiful robes and jewelry for his dear wife. She had been loyal in her love to him, and this was the best way he could think of to show her his gratitude.*

THE TALE OF
MAARUF THE COBBLER
CONTINUES

"You realize we are waiting,
Scheherazade," said Shah Rayar.
"That's the point. Waiting a little helps you to enjoy the
tales more. After all, anticipation enhances feelings."
"You're a genius."
Scheherazade smiled. If he didn't believe that and he was just
flattering her, that was sweet, really. And if he did believe it, who
was she to disabuse him? She began the tale without further ado.

The king and his vizier discussed a plan to entrap
Maaruf the following day. But the next morning the king's
servants came racing to him, lamenting. All of Maaruf's mules
and horses and all of his servants had disappeared. Clearly the
servants had stolen the animals!

None of them guessed, of course, that the horses were jinn
and the mules and servants were the jinni's sons—all in disguise.

The king felt wretched. How could such a thing
happen without anyone noticing? Surely that many beasts
and people had to make noise that woke someone. He
looked on with trepidation as Maaruf appeared and asked
the royal servants why they looked so glum. When Maaruf
learned of the disappearance of the animals and servants,
he wasn't fazed. Those jinn and Abu'l-Sa'adat's sons had to
go back where they came from, of course. He went about
his day, happy as ever.

No reaction could have disturbed the king more. Surely
the vizier was right; this man had to be a magician. So he
invited the vizier and Maaruf to go into the garden with him.

PREVIOUS PAGES:

The clever vizier got Maaruf to drink wine. Soon Maaruf was so inebriated, he held up the magic ring and told the king and his vizier all about the ring jinni.

The king's garden was a paradise of streams that ran among fruit trees where birds sang. The vizier entertained them with stories and jokes, at which he was quite skilled. Maaruf enjoyed himself immensely. Then a servant brought them food and wine. The king drank first. The vizier then filled a glass for Maaruf. But Maaruf, who had been but a humble cobbler before, didn't know what wine was nor how silly it could make one. The vizier recited poem after poem about the virtues of wine, how it can turn grief to joy, how it can make our bodies seem to take flight, how it is liquid gold in restoring the emotions, how even a rock becomes happy when a drop of wine falls on it, how … But it wasn't necessary to keep going, because Maaruf was begging for the wine by now. No sooner did he finish off a glass than the vizier filled it again. Before long, Maaruf was reeling, witless. That's when the vizier cozied up to him. "Tell me the truth, Maaruf. You aren't a rich merchant at all, are you? You're really a king." Oh, this vizier was very clever.

"King? Me? Ha!" And Maaruf told all, right down to the jinni of the ring.

"Let me see that ring," said the vizier.

Maaruf took off the ring and handed it to the vizier, who promptly rubbed it. When the jinni appeared, the vizier pointed at Maaruf and told the jinni to take him away to a desert, with no food or drink, so he could die in painful misery.

The jinni Abu'l-Sa'adat flew away with Maaruf.

"What will you do to me, jinni?" asked the crying Maaruf.

"Exactly what my new master ordered. And you deserve it. What kind of idiot turns over a powerful ring for another to inspect? Idiot idiot idiot." The jinni dropped Maaruf in the driest, most isolated desert.

Scheherazade smelled the damp must that dirt gives off as the morning sun hits it. Her oldest son groaned and opened his eyes. She kissed his forehead.
"The vizier is right; that Maaruf is an idiot," said Shah Rayar.
"But he's a generous, kind idiot," said Dinarzad.
"Agreed. Still, it's right that the vizier has won.
He's seen the truth all along." ✳

Wine as Intoxication

A portrait of the poet Rumi

Many Muslim poets have written poems in praise of wine. This may seem surprising, since Islam prohibits alcohol. However, many of these poets may be using wine as a symbol for other things, such as the way we can feel profoundly changed by new experiences, particularly religious experiences. The poems of the medieval Persian poets Hafiz and Rumi are fine examples of this.

THE TALE OF MAARUF THE COBBLER CONTINUES

"What happens next, Sister?"
Scheherazade put her newborn over her shoulder and burped him.
She waited for Shah Rayar to ask, as well. He didn't.
He clearly thought the story was all laid out now, with no
surprises ahead. Well, she'd show him. And, actually,
she'd better show him fast. Could a man call a woman his
sweet delight and then still kill her? She began.

See?" said the vizier to the king. "I told you he was a fraudster.
I told you magic was afoot. I warned you from the start."

"You did, indeed," said the king. "You are the best vizier ever. Now
pass me that ring so I can have a close look at it."

"Are you a moron?" The vizier spat in the king's face. "I have it now.
I have all the power. There's no reason I should pass it to you ever. In
fact, there's no reason to let you live." He rubbed the ring and the jinni
Abu'l-Sa'adat appeared. "Take this ignoramus of a king and drop him
in the same desert where you dropped Maaruf. They can die together,
cursing one another."

The jinni obeyed, and the king and Maaruf were soon crying side
by side, their stomachs growling with hunger, their throats dry as sand.

The vizier now convened the troops and the royal servants. He told
them about the ring and how he had disposed of Maaruf and their king.
He said they must accept him as ruler or he'd call the jinni to dispose
of them, too. Each one said they accepted him as ruler. After all, the
alternative was sure death.

The vizier had the jinni give the troops robes of honor, for their
allegiance to him. It cost him nothing, so why not? Then he had a
messenger tell the princess he was coming to claim her tonight as his
own wife. The princess cried. She searched for a reason to stall this
hideous action. She had known the vizier was not a good man—she
had sensed this all along. That's why she had refused his offer of
marriage in the first place. She sent back the message that the vizier
must wait till the end of her mourning period for her husband, as

189

the law decreed. The vizier laughed. No law bound him any longer, for he had the jinni. The princess listened to the messenger and a pounding started in her head. She sent a message back that welcomed the vizier. The wicked man was overjoyed. A willing wife was better than an unwilling one.

But did the princess mean that welcome? Of course not. You know she loved Maaruf truly. That love now hammered so loudly in her head that she had to try a trick—a very dangerous trick. She willed herself to be brave.

The vizier came to her that evening. She wore her best robes and flirted with the vizier outrageously. She turned to him coyly and smiled enticingly and her voice was low and caressing.

The vizier responded both because he loved the princess and because he loved himself so much he couldn't imagine that she wasn't sincere, despite the fact that he had as good as killed both her husband and her father. This vizier might have been clever in some ways, but in others he had a clod of dirt for a brain. He approached the princess for a kiss.

She cried. She said there was a man in the ring watching them and the sight of him frightened her. The vizier quickly took off his ring and stuffed it under a pillow. Immediately, the princess kicked the vizier and he fell backward, unconscious. She snatched the ring from under that pillow.

The light of day yellowed the walls. Scheherazade hushed.
"Wicked, stupid vizier," said Dinarzad.
"In some ways, yes, indeed," said Shah Rayar. "Everything
is complicated. I wonder now what the princess will do."
"Save her husband and father, of course," said Dinarzad.
"That's what you would do. That's what I would do.
But we will see what the princess does."

THE TALE OF MAARUF THE COBBLER CONTINUES

"The princess," said Dinarzad. "She has the ring now. What will she do?" "Is everyone listening?" asked Scheherazade. "Yes," said Shah Rayar. "Yes," said their oldest son. Her middle son squirmed beside her and her newborn tightened his finger around her thumb. Scheherazade laughed. She knew they couldn't be listening— or at least not listening with understanding. But she was still grateful; this felt like a real family event.

The princess called out to her servants. Forty maidservants came running. She had them seize the vizier. Then she looked at the ring in her hand and trembled. The vizier had told the soldiers and his servants about the jinni in the ring, and the word had traveled throughout the palace. So she knew there was great power in her hands. But what did it all really mean? She took a deep breath and rubbed the ring.

The jinni Abu'l-Sa'adat appeared and asked what her wish was. He was ghastly. Everyone knew jinn could be taller than trees and more hideous than the ugliest sea creatures, but this apparition made her heart nearly burst. She forced herself to speak. "Put the vizier in prison and shackle him tight." In an instant, jinni and vizier were gone. An instant later the jinni reappeared and asked her next wish. "Where are my husband and father?" The jinni told about the remote desert. "Bring them back. Please." The jinni looked surprised at the word *please*. He disappeared noisily—was that laughter she heard?

Moments later the king and Maaruf were back in the palace. The princess hugged them both. Then they ate their fill and

PREVIOUS PAGES:

The princess faced the phenomenally ugly and scary jinni. She gathered her courage and politely asked him to bring her husband and father back from the desert.

slept long and well, for in their time in the desert they had been too distraught to sleep. The next day the princess told the king to kill the vizier, for he had revealed himself to believe in no law, to be a man of pure wickedness. Maaruf should become vizier in his stead. The king agreed and asked for the ring. The princess had spent the night thinking this through, however. While she loved both husband and father, neither seemed likely to be able to guard the ring properly. "I'll keep it. Should you need anything from it, just ask me and I will ask the jinni."

Then the king and Maaruf presented themselves to the whole royal staff. Everyone was overjoyed to have them back again, for all of them had spent the night fretting, thinking that the vizier had taken the princess as his wife before the legal mourning period was finished.

For the next five years, the entire kingdom was happy, none happier than the princess and Maaruf, for they were now parents of a strong son. Then the old king died and the princess made Maaruf his successor. But soon after, when their son was only five, the princess died of an illness. The ring now belonged to Maaruf once again.

Years later, Maaruf was lying in bed one night when he realized there was a frightful old woman lying beside him. He asked who she was, of course. She answered that she was Dung Fatima. He lit a candle. Now, of course, he could see her teeth, her eyes—yes, this was his first wife. "What are you doing here?"

And so Dung Fatima told her tale of woe. A demon had made her so wretchedly mean to Maaruf, those many years ago. After he disappeared, she realized that and repented. She was so poor then, she had to beg for food. She wandered as a beggar for years, growing ever more miserable. Until the day before, when she sat weeping and a stranger asked her the source of her grief. She told him all and he said he knew this Maaruf. Suddenly, he scooped her up and flew with her here. "Keep me with you, Maaruf. For I am truly repentant. I will be your true wife."

Scheherazade yawned with her first breath of morning.
"I don't trust her," said Dinarzad.
"But will Maaruf?" said Shah Rayar.
Trust. Had Shah Rayar learned to trust? Had Scheherazade?
Scheherazade nestled down among the children and slept. ✸

THE TALE OF MAARUF
THE COBBLER CONCLUDES

"Listen, sweet ones," said Scheherazade.
"We couldn't do otherwise," said Shah Rayar. "You hold us rapt."
That was exactly what Scheherazade wanted to hear.
She began the tale.

King Maaruf had pity on Dung Fatima. He held no love for her anymore—all his love was for his late princess, the mother of his son. But the generosity that had led him to give so many riches to the poor and needy stirred in him constantly. Dung Fatima could never be a real wife to Maaruf, nevertheless, he treated her like a queen, with remarkable clothing and jewels.

Dung Fatima, however, was not satisfied with this. She may have repented her past haglike ways, but she was made of the same stuff she'd always been made of. She was greedy and envious. She hated Maaruf's son for no fault of his own, and the boy, who quickly understood everything, returned the feeling. And she resented every moment that Maaruf spent with the various ladies of the court. Her face bore a deeply grooved scowl.

One day, no more or less full of discontent than other days, it came into Dung Fatima's head to steal the ring. Then she could do whatever she wanted. She could kill Maaruf and make someone else love her. She was a fool, of course. Jinn can bring fortune and jinn can destroy. But jinn cannot make someone love you. Love comes of its own, or it is earned. But it cannot be ordered or bought. Fools can't learn these things, though.

While Maaruf slept, Dung Fatima crept into his bedchamber to steal the ring that she knew he put under his pillow.

But a boy saw her enter the room. He was none other than the prince, the sweet, round-faced son of Maaruf and the princess. Distrust bit at his cheeks, for he was his mother's son and wisdom beyond his years coated his every move. He grabbed his steel sword—at the sight of which his father always laughed, since he was still so young—and stood at the threshold of the chamber.

He witnessed Dung Fatima reach under the pillow and draw out a ring and he understood, poor boy, he understood her wickedness.

She came out of the room and was about to rub the ring, when the boy swung his sword, and she fell dead.

At this commotion, Maaruf sprang from the bed. He praised his son and had Dung Fatima's body properly prepared for burial. Then he sent for that peasant, the one who had run off to the village to bring back lentils for Maaruf and barley for his horse, and made him his vizier. And both lived well, until Maaruf died of old age, praise be to the Almighty, in whose hands we all roll.

*Scheherazade rose from the bed on unsteady feet.
The princess had faced the jinni—how could Scheherazade
feel so wobbly at simply facing her husband? She stood taller,
then knelt tiny and kissed the ground at Shah Rayar's feet.
"Husband, I have entertained you well for 1,001 nights.
Now I have a favor to ask of you."
"Anything," said Shah Rayar.
"These boys, your sons, no one else could raise
them as lovingly as I. Please …"
Shah Rayar put a finger on Scheherazade's lips to hush her.
"Wife, you have not just entertained me for these many nights,
you have educated me, in mind and spirit.
You have nourished my soul. Thank you.
I cherish you, love of my life.
Shall we face the future together, now and forever?"*

You don't need to hear Scheherazade's answer, for you know it. The palace, the town, the whole countryside sang their joy. Shah Rayar showered gifts on everyone. After all, Maaruf was a fool, but only in some ways. Shah Rayar praised the Almighty for the blessings of the 1,001 nights already behind and the wealth of love and trust now and to come.

The Necessity of Hospitality

A man in a tea shop pours a fresh cup of tea for a traveler.

The peasant who fed Maaruf lentils is rewarded by being appointed vizier. This may seem like an extreme gift for such a simple act, but hospitality toward a stranger in need is a teaching of Islam. It is also an important part of Judaism and Christianity, which, like Islam, have their roots in desert lands of the Middle East. In this area, refusal of hospitality could mean death to a traveler. Celtic and Indian cultures, among others, also have a strong tradition of hospitality.

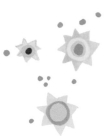

The oldest extant version of the Arabian Nights tales is a Syrian manuscript in Arabic from the 14th century. But some of the stories might be much older than that. Two 10th-century Arab scholars, Al-Mas'ūdī and Ibn al-Nadīm, mention in their writings a collection of stories translated from an older Persian text. And a 12th-century document in the Cairo Synagogue mentions such a collection as well. The Syrian manuscript is known for being written in colloquial language, without the eloquence or complexity of classical Arabic texts. For this reason, scholars believe it might be based on very old folklore, maybe mixed with stories originally in another language (perhaps from Persia, perhaps from India).

In the early 1700s the French scholar Antoine Galland translated the Syrian manuscript into a series of 12 volumes in French. It gained popularity immediately, and several other translations appeared in Europe. In 1984 the Iraqi-American scholar Muhsin Mahdi published the first critical edition of the text in Arabic. And in 1990 the Iraqi scholar Husain Haddawy translated Mahdi's work into English. While there are now several English renditions of at least some of the tales, I worked here mostly with those by Husain Haddawy and by the British scholar Malcolm C. Lyons. Some editors make distinctions between types of magic creatures (a jinni versus an ifrīt); I have chosen to follow Haddawy in not making such a distinction. My work was checked against sources in English, French, and Arabic by my consultant and guide, Professor Selma Zecevic of York University. General information is given in the table on page 203.

Some of the tales modern readers associate with the Arabian Nights were not in the original Syrian text, but were instead added by later writers and translators who wanted to embellish on the traditional tales. I have chosen to mark two such stories as "extra," where these extra tales are told—on the anniversaries of Scheherazade's marriage to Shah Rayar. However, I include one such "orphan tale" among the regular tales, beginning on night 667, "The Tale of Prince Hussain and the Magic Carpet."

The tales in the Arabian Nights are sometimes inconsistent, sometimes mysterious without any obvious coherence, often bawdy, often brutal. They range from the fantastic to the horrific to the erotic, from satire to thriller.

Like many other traditional tales in many other countries and cultures, these stories were not originally tailored specifically to the interests and understanding of children. My goal, however, is to offer stories for the enjoyment of both the child and adult reader. The selection and rendering of tales here reflects that goal.

Nevertheless, I hope to have presented stories that represent the complexities of the overall structure of the tales, that show the wide range of genres found in the original, and that reflect what I see as pervasive values in the tales. I also strove to preserve the sensory and highly textured appeal of the original.

LITERARY LICENSE

Since I tell only a selection of the many stories, I have chosen to organize them in a way that best suits the flow and to adjust their length for matters of pacing. For example, the tale of the ebony horse runs from night 357 through night 370 in the original, but I begin it on night 366 and end on night 370. Likewise, the story of Maaruf the Cobbler begins two days earlier in the original than here in this rendering. I have shortened some of the original tales and lingered over others, and when sources offered variants on a tale, I chose the particulars I found most dramatically coherent to the overall text here. While many details of time and place are included, my attention is on revealing the inherent wisdom of these tales, as well as their complex literary structure, so I chose not to include distinctions that didn't contribute toward these goals. Never, however, did I sacrifice a detail that was important in holding together the logic or emotion of a story. Also, in older texts, not until the final night of the tales does Scheherazade reveal to the king that he has three sons by her. This lack of realism weakened the overall structure of the story as I wanted to tell it; I opted instead for integration of the children in a way that would enhance the relationship between wife and husband. The final license I took involves a name. In the traditional literature, the main character's name is Shahrazad. I use the name Scheherazade, instead, because it is so well known in the United States and because I wanted to keep her name as distinct as possible from Shah Rayar's name.

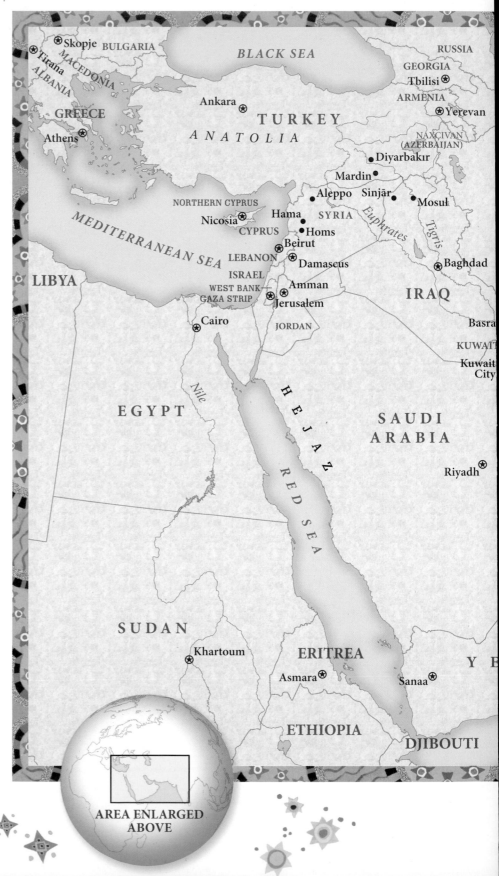

These stories are rich with names. Some refer to places known today, such as the cities Samarqand, Baghdad, and Basra, and the river Tigris. Some refer to historical figures, such as Caliph Harun al-Rashid, who ruled in the late A.D. 700s and early A.D. 800s. So we get a clear idea of where and when a story unfolded.

Other stories mention places vaguely. A city in "far China," for example, might be anywhere in that vast area. Such vagueness is not surprising; knowledge of world geography was limited and changing. Still, the fact that many tales mention the roles of sheikh, caliph, and vizier tells us those took place in Muslim areas after A.D. 600.

Some tales mention fictional cities and islands. Though imaginary, they were often steeped in glories of past times, including Arab, Buddhist, and Zoroastrian traditions. Additionally, translators added stories that they may have envisioned in places more familiar to them. For example, in the early 1700s Antoine Galland produced a French version with a map that includes Europe. The map of Husain Haddawy (from 1950), instead, does not include Europe but does include a greater area of China—as does the map here.

AREA ENLARGED ABOVE

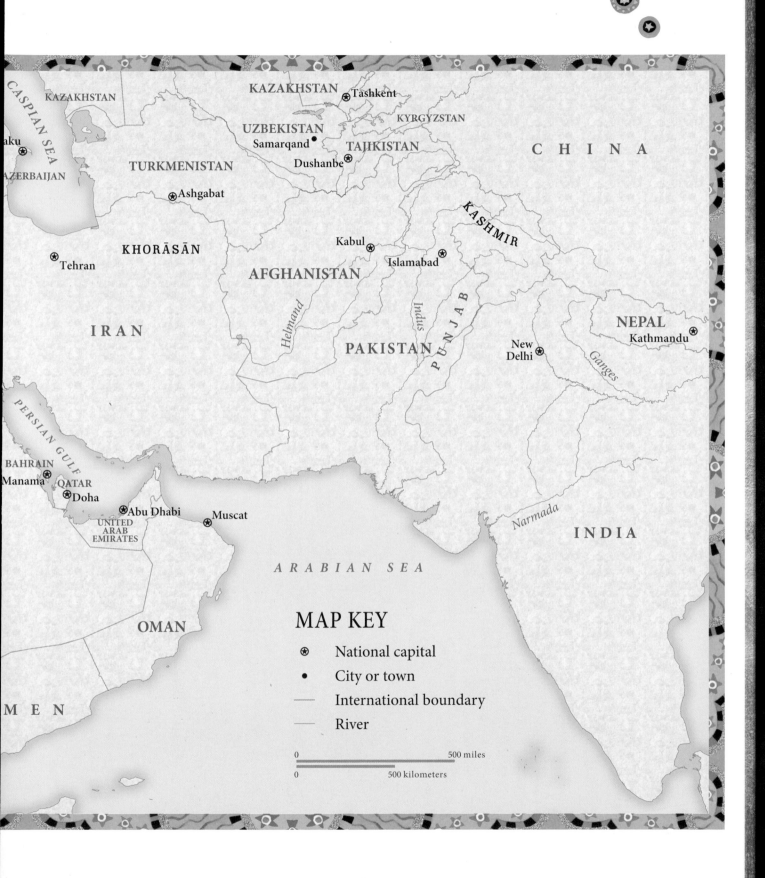

KAZAKHSTAN

CASPIAN SEA

aku

AZERBAIJAN

KAZAKHSTAN

Tashkent

KYRGYZSTAN

UZBEKISTAN

Samarqand

TAJIKISTAN

Dushanbe

CHINA

TURKMENISTAN

Ashgabat

KHORĀSĀN

Tehran

Kabul

AFGHANISTAN

KASHMIR

Islamabad

Helmand

Indus

PUNJAB

PAKISTAN

NEPAL

Kathmandu

New
Delhi

Ganges

IRAN

PERSIAN GULF

BAHRAIN

Manama

QATAR

Doha

Abu Dhabi

Muscat

Narmada

INDIA

UNITED
ARAB
EMIRATES

OMAN

ARABIAN SEA

MEN

MAP KEY

⊛   National capital

•   City or town

—   International boundary

—   River

0 _____ 500 miles

0 _____ 500 kilometers

List of sources consulted by author and guide:

Galland, Antoine (trans.). *Les milles et une nuits (Version Intégrale: 9 tomes)*. Editions la Bibliothèque Digitale, 2012. (abbr. as GLN in table opposite)

Haddawy, Husain (trans.) and Muhsin Mahdi (ed.). *The Arabian Nights, Part I*. New York and London: W. W. Norton & Company, 2008. (abbr. as HH I in table opposite)

Haddawy, Husain (trans.) and Muhsin Mahdi (ed.). *Sindbad: And Other Stories From the Arabian Nights*. New York and London: W. W. Norton & Company, 2008. (abbr. as HH II in table opposite)

Lyons, Malcolm C. (trans.), Ursula Lyons (trans.), and Robert Irwin (intro.). *The Arabian Nights: Tales of 1,001 Nights, Vols. I–III*. New York and London: Penguin Classics, 2010. (abbr. as LYN in table opposite)

Marzolph, Ulrich, and Richard van Leewen. *The Arabian Nights Encyclopedia*. Vols. 1–2. ABC-CL10, 2004.

List of sources in Arabic consulted by guide:

Bulaq, Matba`at Bulaq (ed.). *Alf laylah wa-laylah*, Vols. I–II. Cairo, Egypt: Egyptian Government, 1835. (Includes the material from the Syrian manuscript plus additional tales) (abbr. as BLQ in table opposite)

Macnaghten, W. H. S. (ed.). *Alf laylah wa-laylah,* Vols. I–IV. Calcutta: Thacker, 1835–1842. (The most extensive manuscript, including the tales from the Syrian manuscript plus additional tales) (abbr. as CLC II in table opposite)

Muhsin Mahdi (ed.). *Kitāb alf laylah wa-laylah: min uṣūlihi al-'Arabīyah al-ūlā,* Vols. I–III. Leiden, The Netherlands: E.J. Brill, 1984. (Critical edition of the 14th-century Syrian manuscript) (abbr. as MM in table opposite)

Bibliography for the sidebars:

Sidebar for The Tale of Shah Rayar and Shah Zaman:
Schimmel, Annemarie. *The Mystery of Numbers*. Oxford: Oxford University Press (1993): 93–96.

Sidebar for Night 2:
Peters, F. E. *The Hajj: The Muslim Pilgrimage to Mecca and the Holy Places*. Princeton: Princeton University Press (1994): 29–32.

Sidebar for Night 4:
King, David A. "Ibn Yūnus' Very Useful Tables for Reckoning Time by the Sun." *Archive for History of Exact Sciences*, Vol. 10, no. 3 (1973): 342–394.

Sidebar for Night 6:
Richter-Bernburg, Lutz. "Abu Bakr Muhammad al-Razi's (Rhazes) Medical Works." *Medicina nei secoli*, Vol. 6, no. 2 (1993): 377–392.

Sidebar for Night 20:
Ahmad ibn Yahya al-Baladhuri. *Futuh al-Buldan*. Cairo: Dar al-Nashr li-l-Jami'in (1993): 353.

El-Hibri, Tayeb. *Reinterpreting Islamic Historiography: Harun Al-Rashid and the Narrative of the Abbasid Caliphate*. Cambridge: Cambridge University Press, 1999.

Sidebar for Night 23:
Rashad, Hoda, Magued Osman, and Farzaneh Roudi-Fahimi. *Marriage in the Arab World*. Population Reference Bureau (PRB), 2005.

Sidebar for Night 52:
Bejtić, Alija. "The Idea of Beautiful in the Sources of Islam." *Prilozi za Orijentalnu Filologiju*, Vol. 50 (2000): 113–136.

Brewer, Derek S. "The Ideal of Feminine Beauty in Medieval Literature, Especially 'Harley Lyrics,' Chaucer, and Some Elizabethans." *The Modern Language Review* (1955): 257–269.

Thornhill, Randy, and Steven W. Gangestad. "Human facial beauty." *Human Nature,* Vol. 4, no. 3 (1993): 237–269.

Sidebar for Night 53:
Al-Issa, Ihsan (ed.). *Al-Junūn: Mental Illness in the Islamic World*. International Universities Press, Inc., 2000.

Sidebar for Night 56:
Bosworth, C. E. "A pioneer Arabic Encyclopedia of the Sciences: al-Khwārizmī's Keys of the Sciences," *Isis,* Vol. 4, no. 1 (1963): 97–111.

Sidebar 1 for Night 365:
Köksel, Hamit, and Buket Cetiner. "Future of Grain Science Series: Grain Science and Industry in Turkey: Past, Present, and Future." *Cereal Foods World*, Vol. 60, no. 2 (2015): 90–96.

Sidebar 2 for Night 365:
Carroll, Cain, and Revital Carroll. *Mudras of India: A Comprehensive Guide to the Hand Gestures of Yoga and Indian Dance*. Singing Dragon, 2012.

Sidebar for Night 367:
Chauvin, Victor. "Pacolet et les Mille et une Nuits." *Wallonia,* Vol. 6 (1898): 5–19.

Marzolph, Ulrich, and Richard van Leeuwen. "The Ebony Horse" in *The Arabian Nights Encyclopedia,* Vol. 1. ABC-CLIO (2004): 174.

Osborn, Marijane. "The Squire's 'Steed of Brass' as Astrolabe: Some Implications for The Canterbury Tales," *Hermeneutics and Medieval Culture,* Patrick J. Gallacher and Helen Damico (eds.) Albany: State University of New York Press (1989), 121–124.

Sidebar for Night 368:
Ansari, Nazia. *The Islamic Garden*. Department of Landscape Architecture; CEPT University, 2011. Available at: academia.edu/1861364/ Origin_of_Islamic_Gardens

Sidebar for Night 370:
Sherman, Josepha. *Storytelling: An Encyclopedia of Mythology and Folklore* (Google ebook), 5. (for discussion of the etymology of "abracadabra")

Uchino, Bert N., John T. Cacioppo, and Janice K. Kiecolt-Glaser. "The Relationship Between Social Support and Physiological Processes: A Review With Emphasis on Underlying Mechanisms and Implications for Health." *Psychological Bulletin,* Vol. 119, no. 3 (1996): 488–531.

Sidebar for Night 538:
Thesiger, Wilfred. *The Marsh Arabs*. New York: Penguin, 2007.

Sidebar for Night 540:
Scott, Derek A. "A Review of the Status of the Breeding Waterbirds in Iran in the 1970s." *Podoces*, Vol. 2, no. 1 (2007): 1–21.

Sidebar for Night 541:
Simpson, George Gaylord. *Horses: The Story of the Horse Family in the Modern World and Through Sixty Million Years of History*. New York: Anchor Books, 1951.

Sidebar for Night 543:
Kemp, Christopher. *Floating Gold: A Natural (and Unnatural) History of Ambergris*. University of Chicago Press, 2012.

Sidebar for Night 544:
Keijl, Guido O., and Tom M. van der Have. "Observations on Marine Mammals in Southern Iran, January 2000." *Zoology in the Middle East,* Vol. 26, no. 1 (2002): 37–40.

Nixon, Roy W. "The Date Palm—'Tree of Life' in the Subtropical Deserts."*Economic Botany,* Vol. 5, no. 3 (1951): 274–301.

Sidebar for Night 667:
Carmean, Kelli. *Spider Woman Walks This Land: Traditional Cultural Properties and the Navajo Nation*. Rowman Altamira, 2002.

Jacobsen, Charles. *Oriental Rugs: A Complete Guide*. Tuttle Publishing, 2013.

Sidebar for Night 668:
Cutter, Irving S., and Henry R. Viets. "A Short History of Midwifery." *The American Journal of the Medical Sciences,* Vol. 250, no. 2 (1965): 236.

Merli, Claudia. "Muslim Midwives Between Traditions and Modernities. Being and Becoming a Bidan Kampung in Satun Province, Southern Thailand." *Moussons. Recherche en sciences humaines sur l'Asie du Sud-Est* 15 (2010): 121–135.

Sidebar 1 for Night 730:
Shirazi, Faegheh. *The Veil Unveiled: The Hijab in Modern Culture.* Gainesville: University Press of Florida, 2001.

Von Grunebaum, Gustave E. *Medieval Islam: A Study in Cultural Orientation.* University of Chicago Press, 2010.

Sidebar 2 for Night 730:
Amundsen, Darrel W. *Medicine, Society, and Faith in the Ancient and Medieval Worlds.* Baltimore, MD: Johns Hopkins University Press, 1996.

Winkelman, Michael James. "Shamans and Other 'Magico-Religious' Healers: A Cross-Cultural Study of Their Origins, Nature, and Social Transformations." *Ethos,* Vol. 18, no. 3 (1990): 308–352.

Sidebar for Night 992:
Baram, Uzi, and Lynda Carroll (eds.). *A Historical Archaeology of the Ottoman Empire: Breaking New Ground.* Springer, 2000.

Salloum, Habeeb, Leila Salloum Elias, and Muna Salloum. *Scheherazade's Feasts: Foods of the Medieval Arab World.* Philadelphia: University of Pennsylvania Press, 2014.

Sato, Tsugitaka. *Sugar in the Social Life of Medieval Islam.* Leiden: Brill, 2015.

Sidebar for Night 996:
Lapidus, Ira M. *A History of Islamic Societies.* Cambridge University Press, 2002.

Sidebar for Night 998:
Banani, Amin, Richard Hovannisian, and Georges Sabagh (eds.). *Poetry and Mysticism in Islam: The Heritage of Rumi,* Vol. 11. Cambridge University Press, 1994.

Meisami, Julie Scott. "Allegorical Gardens in the Persian Poetic Tradition: Nezami, Rumi, Hafez." *International Journal of Middle East Studies,* Vol. 17, no. 2 (1985): 229–260.

Saeidi, Ali, and Tim Unwin. "Persian Wine Tradition and Symbolism: Evidence From the Medieval Poetry of Hafiz." *Journal of Wine Research,* Vol. 15, no. 2 (2004): 97–114.

Sidebar for Night 1,001:
Koenig, John. *New Testament Hospitality.* Philadelphia: Fortress Press, 1985.

Miller, William T. *Mysterious Encounters at Mamre and Jabbok.* Chico, CA: Scholars Press, 1984.

Walzer, Michael. *Spheres of Justice: A Defense of Pluralism and Equality.* New York: Basic Books, 1983.

ORIGINS OF THE TALES AND SOURCES USED IN THE COMPARATIVE TEXTUAL ANALYSIS

TALES	ORIGIN	ARABIC SOURCES	TRANSLATIONS
Shah Rayar & Shah Zaman	Syrian Manuscript	MM, CLC II	HH I, LYN
The Donkey, the Ox & the Merchant	Syrian Manuscript	MM, CLC II	HH I, LYN
The Merchant & the Jinni	Syrian Manuscript	MM, CLC II	HH I, LYN
The First Sheikh	Syrian Manuscript	MM, CLC II	HH I, LYN
The Second Sheikh	Syrian Manuscript	MM, CLC II	HH I, LYN
The Third Sheikh's Story & The Tale of the Fisherman & the Jinni	Syrian Manuscript	MM, CLC II	HH I, LYN
King Yunan & the Sage Duban	Syrian Manuscript	MM, CLC II	HH I, LYN
The Husband & the Parrot & the Ogress	Syrian Manuscript	MM, CLC II	HH I, LYN
The Three Apples	Syrian Manuscript	MM, CLC II	HH I, LYN
The Vizier's Two Sons	Syrian Manuscript	MM, CLC II	HH I, LYN
Qamar al-Zaman	Only a few pages in the Syrian Manuscript; full versions in BLQ, CLC I and CLC II	BLQ, CLC II	LYN
Ali Baba & the Forty Thieves	Orphan Tale	CLC II	GLN, HH II, LYN
The Ebony Horse	Orphan Tale	CLC II	GLN, HH II, LYN
Sindbad the Sailor	No full Arabic version exists prior to the 18th century.	CLC II	GLN, HH II, LYN
Prince Hussain & the Magic Carpet	Orphan Tale. First published by GLN under the title "Histoire du prince Ahmed et de la fee Pari-Banou"		GLN
Aladdin	Orphan Tale	CLC II	GLN, HH II, LYN
Maaruf the Cobbler	(most probably) Egyptian Manuscript	BLQ, CLC II	LYN

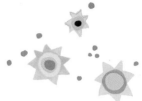

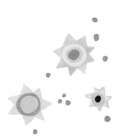

For guidance and encouragement throughout the entire process of putting together this book, enormous gratitude goes to Associate Professor Selma Zecevic of the Department of Humanities at York University in Toronto. The author and illustrator also thank the National Geographic team who worked on this project for their resourcefulness, energy, and wisdom: Karen Ang, Christina Ascani, Lewis Bassford, Callie Broaddus, Rebekah Cain, Shira Evans, Rachel Faulise, Erica Green, Grace Hill, Alix Inchausti, Priyanka Lamichhane, Angela Modany, and David Seager.

Since 1888, the National Geographic Society has funded more than 12,000 research, exploration, and preservation projects around the world. The Society receives funds from National Geographic Partners LLC, funded in part by your purchase. A portion of the proceeds from this book supports this vital work. To learn more, visit www.natgeo.com/info.

For more information, visit nationalgeographic.com, call 1-800-647-5463, or write to the following address:
National Geographic Partners
1145 17th Street N.W.
Washington, D.C. 20036-4688 U.S.A.

Visit us online at nationalgeographic.com/books

For librarians and teachers: ngchildrensbooks.org

More for kids from National Geographic: kids.nationalgeographic.com

For information about special discounts for bulk purchases, please contact National Geographic Books Special Sales: ngspecsales@ngs.org

For rights or permissions inquiries, please contact National Geographic Books Subsidiary Rights: ngbookrights@ngs.org

NATIONAL GEOGRAPHIC and Yellow Border Design are trademarks of the National Geographic Society, used under license.

Art Directed by Callie Broaddus and David Seager

Trade hardcover ISBN: 978-1-4263-2540-3
Reinforced library edition ISBN: 978-1-4263-2541-0

Printed in Hong Kong
16/THK/1

ILLUSTRATIONS CREDITS

All artwork by Christina Balit unless otherwise noted below.
Cover (LO), Nata-Lia/Shutterstock; 10 (LE), Carmen Martinez Banus/Getty Images; 17 (RT), Duby Tal/Albatross/Alamy; 23 (RT), The Image Bank/Getty Images; 29 (RT), Mary Evans Picture Library/Alamy; 34 (LE), Andreykuzmin/Dreamstime; 40 (LE), Ivy Close Images/Alamy; 47 (LE), Getty Images; 52 (LE), Dimitri Vervitsiotis/Getty Images; 60 (LE), Abam Jiwa AL-Hadi/Getty Images; 64 (LE), Granger, NYC—All rights reserved; 71 (RT), Stock4B-RF/Getty Images; 77 (CTR RT), Said Khatib/AFP/Getty Images; 84 (CTR LE), ephotocorp/Alamy; 89 (RT), Moment RM/Getty Images; 94 (LE), Matyas Rehak/Shutterstock; 102 (LE), Rhapsode/Getty Images; 107 (RT), AFP/Getty Images; 115 (RT), Jose B. Ruiz/NPL/Minden Pictures; 118 (LE), Gallo Images/Getty Images; 125 (RT), Waterframe/Getty Images; 131 (RT), Oleg Zaslavsky/Shutterstock; 136 (LE), Natig Aghayev/Shutterstock; 144 (LE), Jodi Cobb/National Geographic Creative; 153 (RT), Vetta/Getty Images; 165 (RT), Science Source/Getty Images; 170 (LE), Robert Harding World Imagery/Getty Images; 182 (LE), Vetta/Getty Images; 188 (LE), Granger, NYC; 196 (LE), Alex Treadway/NG Creative